The Eames-Erskine Case

A Chief Inspector Pointer Mystery

By A. E. Fielding

Originally published in 1925

The Eames-Erskine Case

© 2014 Resurrected Press
www.ResurrectedPress.com

Published by Intrepid Ink, LLC

Intrepid Ink, LLC provides full publishing services to authors of fiction and non-fiction books, eBooks and websites. From editing to formatting, to publishing, to marketing, Intrepid Ink gets your creative works into the hands of the people who want to read them.
Find out more at www.IntrepidInk.com.

ISBN 13: 978-1-937022-76-1

Printed in the United States of America

Other Resurrected Press Books in
The Chief Inspector Pointer Mystery Series

RESURRECTED PRESS CLASSIC MYSTERY CATALOGUE

Journeys into Mystery
Travel and Mystery in a More Elegant Time

The Edwardian Detectives
Literary Sleuths of the Edwardian Era

Gems of Mystery
Lost Jewels from a More Elegant Age

Anne Austin
One Drop of Blood
The Black Pigeon
Murder at Bridge

E. C. Bentley
Trent's Last Case: The Woman in Black

Ernest Bramah
Max Carrados Resurrected:
The Detective Stories of Max Carrados

Agatha Christie
The Secret Adversary
The Mysterious Affair at Styles

Octavus Roy Cohen
Midnight

Freeman Wills Croft
The Ponson Case
The Pit Prop Syndicate

Whose Body?

Sir William Magnay
The Hunt Ball Mystery

Mabel and Paul Thorne
The Sheridan Road Mystery

Louis Tracy
The Strange Case of Mortimer Fenley
The Albert Gate Mystery
The Bartlett Mystery
The Postmaster's Daughter
The House of Peril
The Sandling Case: What Would You Have Done?

Charles Edmonds Walk
The Paternoster Ruby

John R. Watson
The Mystery of the Downs
The Hampstead Mystery

Edgar Wallace
The Daffodil Mystery
The Crimson Circle

Carolyn Wells
Vicky Van
The Man Who Fell Through the Earth
In the Onyx Lobby
Raspberry Jam
The Clue
The Room with the Tassels
The Vanishing of Betty Varian
The Mystery Girl
The White Alley
The Curved Blades

FOREWORD

The period between the First and Second World Wars
has rightly been called the "Golden Age of British
Mysteries." It was during this period that Agatha
Christie, Dorothy L. Sayers, and Margery Allingham first
turned their pens to crime. On the male side, the era saw
such writers as Anthony Berkeley, John Dickson Carr,
and Freeman Wills Crofts join the ranks of writers of
detective fiction. The genre was immensely popular at
the time on both sides of the Atlantic, and by the end of
the 1930's one out of every four novels published in
Britain was a mystery.

While Agatha Christie and a few of her peers have
remained popular and in print to this day, the same
cannot be said of all the authors of this period. With so
many mysteries published in the period, it is inevitable
that many of them would become obscure or worse,
forgotten, often with no justification than changing public
tastes. The case of Archibald Fielding is one such, an
author, who though popular enough to have a career
spanning two decades and more than two dozen
mysteries has become such a cipher that his, or as seems
more likely, her real identity as become as much a
mystery as the books themselves.

The books attributed to Archibald Fielding, A. E.
Fielding, or Archibald E. Fielding, are quintessential
Golden Age British mysteries. They include all the
attributes, the country houses, the tangled webs of
relationships, the somewhat feckless cast of characters
who seem to have nothing better to do with themselves
than to murder or be murdered. Their focus is on a
middle class and upper class struggling to find

themselves in the new realities of the post war era while still trying to live the lifestyle of the Edwardian era. Things are never as they seem, red herrings are distributed liberally through the pages as are the clues that will ultimately lead to the solution of "the puzzle," for the British mysteries of this period are centered on the puzzle element which both the reader and the detective must solve before the last page.

A majority of the Fielding mysteries involve the character of Chief Inspector Pointer. Unlike the eccentric Belgian Hercule Poirot, the flamboyant Lord Peter Wimsey, or the somewhat mysterious Albert Campion, Pointer is merely a competent, sometimes clever, occasionally intuitive policeman. And unlike as with Inspector French in the stories of Freeman Wills Croft, the emphasis is on the mystery itself, not the process of detection. While the early books fall plainly in the "humdrum" school with Pointer appearing almost immediately and much of story revolving on the business of tracking down various clues, the later novels are much more concerned with the characters surrounding the mystery. Pointer is much less center stage, arriving instead at mid-book to clean up the pieces and insure that the guilty do not escape justice. It is, perhaps, this lack of focus on the detective, which has caused the works of Fielding to fade away while the likes of Poirot seem to attract the interest of each new generation.

The Eames-Erskine Case is the first of the nearly two-dozen mysteries that were to feature Chief Inspector Pointer of Scotland Yard. Unlike many of the later novels, Pointer shows up almost immediately, appearing in the second paragraph when he is called in to investigate the suspicious death of a young man whose body has been discovered in the wardrobe of a London hotel room. Though at first the death is assumed to be a suicide, the chief inspector has his suspicions, suspicions that are to lead his investigation across two continents and which are to uncover multiple crimes dating back years. Though only the author's second novel, it already shows Fielding's talent for introducing unexpected twists in the plot.

Despite their obscurity, the mysteries of Archibald Fielding, whoever he or she might have been, are well written, well crafted examples of the form, worthy of the interest of the fans of the genre. It is with pleasure, then, that Resurrected Press presents this new edition of *The Eames-Erskine Case* and others in the series to its readers.

About the Author

The identity of the author is as much a mystery as the plots of the novels. Two dozen novels were published from 1924 to 1944 as by Archibald Fielding, A. E. Fielding, or Archibald E. Fielding, yet the only clue as to the real author is a comment by the American publishers, H.C. Kinsey Co. that A. E. Fielding was in reality a "middle-aged English woman by the name of Dorothy Feilding whose peacetime address is Sheffield Terrace, Kensington, London, and who enjoys gardening." Research on the part of John Herrington has uncovered a person by that name living at 2 Sheffield Terrace from 1932-1936. She appears to have moved to Islington in 1937 after which she disappears. To complicate things, some have attributed the authorship to Lady Dorothy Mary Evelyn Moore nee Feilding (1889-1935), however, a grandson of Lady Dorothy denied any family knowledge of such authorship. The archivist at Collins, the British publisher, reports that any records of A. Fielding were presumably lost during WWII. Birthdates have been given variously as 1884, 1889, and 1900. Unless new information comes to light, it would appear that the real authorship must remain a mystery.

Greg Fowlkes
Editor-In-Chief
Resurrected Press
www.ResurrectedPress.com

CHAPTER ONE

The door opened noiselessly, and four men came in. They were in plain clothes, and one carried a large box.

"Evening," said the first. "I am Chief Inspector Pointer from New Scotland Yard. These are detectives Watts, Miller and Lester. What's wrong?"

"I 'phoned," a tall young man answered crisply. "I am the manager of the hotel. This is Mr. Beale, an American gentleman to whom this room was let a couple of hours ago. It really belongs to a young fellow who is away for the week-end, but as there was no other room available we assigned it to this gentleman for the one night. Mr. Beale has just told me that there is something wrong about the wardrobe you see there. Kindly investigate that large knot-hole in the back for yourself, Inspector."

The Chief Inspector peered at the hole indicated, ran a finger lightly around it, and inserted it as gently as a mother feeling her baby's tooth. His face showed no change of expression, but, stepping back, he looked the piece of furniture over with the meticulous care of a would-be purchaser hoping to find a flaw, before he got on a chair and examined the top.

"Miller, take your coat off and be doing something outside. See that no one lingers, and notice if any of the doors along the corridor are open."

"Yes, sir." The man vanished.

"The wardrobe evidently stood back against the wall. I take it that it hasn't been tampered with in any way before you rang us up, Mr. Manager?"

"Not by me. This gentleman called me in because he

fancied that there was something wrong."

The Chief Inspector looked Mr. Beale over almost as carefully as he had the wardrobe. He did not strike the police officer as the kind of man to be occupying just such an apartment, for the room looked simple, and Mr. Beale did not,—not in the least. "Did you do anything to it, sir?"

The well-dressed, well-manicured, middle-aged man folded his hands over his ample front, pursed up a cruel mouth, and shook his head. "No, Chief, not beyond moving it out and feeling around through that gaping hole same as yourself." His voice wrapped the Stars and Stripes around him.

"I'd be obliged, gentlemen, if you will remain quite still for a few minutes. Lester, I want the usual flash-light photos."

"Yes, sir," and the photographer got to work. The exposures were quickly made.

"Now, then, help Watts to lift the top off, and we'll get the wardrobe on its side. Gently does it."

"Ah-h-h!" came from the two men watching, and the manager made an impulsive forward movement.

"Stand back, sir!" The Chief Inspector's voice was sharp. "Now, another flashlight, Lester."

When this was done, the Chief Inspector unobtrusively picked up a wax vesta which had tumbled out from the wardrobe while the huddled figure inside was lifted on to the bed.

"Good God!" The manager stared at the placid young face bent stiffly to one side: "it's the young fellow himself,—Eames—who took this room hardly a week ago. Why, I had a telephone message from him at five o'clock saying that he was going out of town for the week-end."

"And now it's nine-thirty. Humph! You can positively identify him?"

"Positively."

The Chief Inspector took a letter which one of his men had just found in the dead man's coat pocket. He examined it closely before holding it out to the manager.

"It's for you, sir."

The manager started back, and turned a little pale. He did not seem to care for the task of opening it, but after a moment's hesitation he ripped the envelope and read in a low voice:

"Enterprise Hotel,
Aug. 4th.
Sir,
Enclosed please find £10 to pay for my bill, and the cheapest funeral possible. It may save time and trouble to know that I have just taken an overdose of morphia, after 'phoning to you to let my room stay as it is until Monday. I am now about to fasten myself into my temporary coffin. I have nothing left to live for. I only regret on your behalf that chance has made your hotel my stepping-off plank. For both our sakes do your best to keep the matter quiet.
Faithfully yours,
Reginald Eames."

"Suicide!" The manager's voice sounded almost triumphant.

Mr. Beale said nothing. With his hands in his pockets he stood staring down at the quiet figure.

"You recognise him too, sir?" Pointer appeared to have eyes in the back of his head, for he stood with his face turned away from the American, still scrutinising the dead man's letter.

Mr. Beale's small, piercing eyes, which gleamed like mica behind the circles of his horn pince-nez, went dull.

"No, Chief, no. I'm a stranger to this wicked little village of yours. I was just wondering what it is that makes young men throw away their lives so easily for the first pretty face that comes along. I suppose there'll be a girl at the bottom of this case, too." He turned away. "Any objection to a cigar all round?"

"Not unless they're lit," and the Chief Inspector accepted one, too. The manager came out of his abstraction. He had been wondering, among other things, how to give the news of the occurrence to the Press in its least interesting form. "Perhaps you could leave taking him away till one o'clock?"

"Very good, sir. You'll find that we try to be as little in the way as possible. Did he have anything in your safe?"

"No, nothing."

"Now, gentlemen, if you'll both step into another room, I'll join you later to hear any further particulars you can give me. First, sir, kindly point out anything that is yours."

Mr. Beale took up his top-coat and umbrella, while the manager picked up a bag. Watts looked all three over very carefully inside and out, his superior lending a casual hand.

When the police officers were alone they rapidly finished the undressing of the young man. He seemed barely thirty.

"Done no manual work," Watts laid a hand down gently, "or—I'm not so sure. But at any rate not a dandy. No manicuring."

"Has been in the habit of wearing a ring for years, judging by that oval mark, very likely a signet ring. Found one in his pockets?" But nothing was found in the young man's pockets except a handkerchief marked R.E., a fountain pen, a pencil—at whose point the Superintendent gazed meditatively—the keys of the wardrobe and the chest of drawers, and a watch and chain.

The Chief Inspector held the inside pocket of the waistcoat to the light.

"Look at that shiny place. He's been in the habit of carrying a note-book there."

"Very poor watch, and most expensive chain," Watts remarked significantly, "wonder if he's some kind of a hotel-rat?"

"His clothes aren't flashy," Pointer pointed out, "good material and cut, though well-worn. Ah, here's the doctor!"

The surgeon took but a few minutes before he straightened the sheet again. "Dead not less than four hours—and not more than five." He put his thermometer away.

"Died between four-thirty and five-thirty," wrote the police officers. "Cause of death, doctor?"

"Morphia, as far as I can judge at present, and he didn't make the mistake of taking too little. Everything points to a tremendous dose. He drank it probably; so far I've seen no punctures. Autopsy will tell more on Monday," and the Doctor bustled off.

The two detectives turned to the wardrobe.

"Those back panels have been screwed on very badly, sir, and as for this little brass bolt on the door inside — it's a shocking sight." Watts' father was a cabinet- maker and he spoke as an expert.

"Just so. The odd thing is that both seem done by the same bungler! Pointer was looking carefully at the two specimens of handicraft. "Now Mr. Eames is obviously to be held responsible for the addition of the bolt which was to serve instead of locking the door on the inside, but he could hardly have been interested in the back panels, one would think."

It was quite half an hour later, when, leaving his subordinate at work, the Chief Inspector stepped out into the little corridor.

Miller rose to his feet and pointed at the next door but one to the room the Chief Inspector had just left. "That door was ajar, sir, when I came out. It's stayed shut since."

Pointer glanced at it. "Number eleven," he registered to himself. The room he had just left was number fourteen. There was no number thirteen in the hotel.

"The manager said if you'd go down to the lounge, find knock on the brown door to the right of the stairs, sir, he and the other gent, would be expecting you Miller set to work again, extracting tacks from the carpet and replacing them carefully.

Pointer seemed to have a good deal of difficulty in finding his way. He roamed around the service-stairs which passed not far from number fourteen, and even opened a door on the ground floor leading from them into the street. Here a couple of muddy foot-prints kept him busy for some minutes. He measured and traced them before he closed the door noiselessly, and experimented with its locks and bolts. Only then did he drift by a series of detours into the lounge and the manager's private suite.

The manager poured out a whisky and soda, which the Chief Inspector left untouched.

"I'm afraid I must take each of your depositions separately, gentlemen. I'll take your statement first, sir, as I understand it was you who called the manager to No. 14." Pointer got out his book and rapidly entered the date, August 4th—ten-thirty p.m.—Enterprise Hotel, while the manager left to look up his registers.

"My name, Chief, is Augustus P. Beale. I'm a sub-editor of the *New York Universe.*" The police officer inclined his head as though in homage to the mighty journal's name.

"Came over on the *Campania* for a year's holiday last month,—by the way, here's my passport, but don't tell me that photo's a good one. We landed July 20th. I've been in Paris most of the time since with some friends, got lonely when they left, and came to London. Arrived this morning by the boat train—Calais-Dover—and found everything full. Worked my way around to the Enterprise, and was told that here, too, every room was taken. Threw myself upon the manager's breast with my credentials in both hands, and begged him to take pity on my grey hairs and save me from a bench in the park. He thought awhile, and, taking me by the hand, with a heavenly smile, led me to a room, explained that it really belonged to a man who was spending the weekend in the country, but that if I would let it go at that for one night he would fix me up something better in the morning. I accepted with tears of gratitude, and after dinner in their restaurant settled myself down before a gas-fire with a cup of coffee. It was pouring, as you know, and I sat warming my toes and putting down my expenses. A shilling rolled under the wardrobe and I fished for it with my umbrella. Couldn't get it, then I tried to move the wardrobe out. Its weight surprised me. However, I got it away from the wall at last and recovered my shilling. As I straightened up, the light from the little electric torch I was using fell full into the knot-hole, and I caught a glimpse of what certainly looked like a piece of human skin,—bit of a cheek. I touched it. There's only one thing in the world that feels like that, and that's a dead body. That was enough for me. I went off post-haste for the manager, found him by good luck just outside in the corridor, and brought him back. He sent for you. That's all."

"Thank you, sir." The Chief Inspector handed back the passport. "May I ask the names of your friends in Paris, though I don't suppose for a moment that there'll be any need to use the addresses."

"I only stayed part of the time at private houses. Part of the time I put up at the Crillon. I'm afraid I don't just see my way to giving you my friends' names. You ask about me at the Embassy, Chief: they'll set your mind at rest."

"Thank you, sir, but my mind isn't uneasy. All these questions are only part of the routine." The Chief Inspector smiled that cheery smile of his which the London underworld dreaded more than any frown. "And now, this afternoon—let me see, where did you say you were?"

"The boat didn't get in till about five. The rest of the time till I arrived here about half-past six I spent in taxis driving from hotel to hotel. Anything else, Chief?"

The Chief Inspector assured him that there was nothing else, and suggested that he might like to try one of the very comfortable chairs in the lounge, and that should he meet the manager would he mind asking him to step into his own sitting-room again.

The manager's story was brevity itself. He told of Beale's arrival "about half-past six," his appeal to him to get him some sort of a shelter on such a night. "I believe he offered to share the dog's kennel provided the beast didn't bite. Incidentally, he told me who he was. Of course, I wanted to do my best for such a client, and thought of the only vacant room in the house,—No. 14. It was fresh in my mind, for I had been talking to the booking clerk when the 'phone came through saying that Mr. Eames would be away over the week-end. Of course as a rule we shouldn't dream of letting anyone else occupy a room under such circumstances, but—"

"One moment: who answered the 'phone?"

"The booking-clerk."

"Thank you, sir. Well, so you took Mr. Beale to No. 14. Did you have the room freshly done up for him—I mean, fresh towels and so on?"

"Of course."

"And then?"

"I saw him at dinner in our restaurant, and said a word to the head waiter, then I saw no more of him till he stopped me in the corridor and told me that there was a dead man in his wardrobe."

"Could you repeat his exact words?"

"'Excuse me, Mr. Manager, but do you know that someone's left a dead man in the wardrobe of that room you let me have?'"

"How did he look? Excited? Frightened?"

The manager thought a moment. "Excited, I should say, and trying not to show it."

"And now you, sir, where were you this afternoon?"

The manager sat up.

"But look here, Inspector,—why, good God,—I thought it was as clear a case of suicide—" The manager's eyes were almost out of his head.

"Bless you, sir, ten to one this is all only a matter of

form. We always do it. Police routine, you know."

"I see. Yes, I see." But obviously it took the manager some effort to focus his mental gaze. "Well, I was all over the place." He named his various movements.

The Chief Inspector's pen flew over the paper.

"That's all, thank you, sir. Will you send me the booking-clerk—unless I'm taking up this room?"

The manager's one desire was that the Chief Inspector should stay in seclusion. Once let a suspicion get about in the hotel that the police were turned loose in it—he thought of them as he might have of the elements of fire or water—and gone would be the hum and stir as of a prosperous hive which rose from all around them.

The story told by the booking-clerk was equally simple.

"Eight days ago—on July twenty-fifth,—about noon, a young man carrying a bag had come into the hotel and asked for a single room on the first floor facing the front. None of these were free for the moment. He had refused to take another, had deposited ten shillings, and asked them to keep him the first one that should be free, giving his name as Reginald Eames. He was back about six o'clock. Meanwhile one had fallen vacant—number fourteen. He took it without looking at it, and registered."

"All your rooms are the same price, I believe?"

"Yes, all. Here's his entry."

The Chief Inspector read, "Reginald Eames. Dentist. Manchester." He compared the writing carefully with the letter found on the dead man.

"I shall want to have that signature photographed," was his only comment. "Well?"

"Well, that's all. I saw him about a bit. He spent all his time in the lounge. This morning I met him at lunch in the restaurant. Seems funny that a man should bother with a meal a few hours before he intends to chuck the whole thing."

The Chief Inspector was not interested in philosophic abstractions. "When did he lunch?"

"I entered at half-past one, just as he was leaving. That's everything I know about the chap except that someone 'phoned up at five o'clock to say that Mr. Eames, of room number fourteen, wished to let us know that he wouldn't be back till Monday morning, as he was spending the week-end in the country with a friend."

"Are you sure of the time?"

The clerk shook his head. "Only there or thereabouts. It wasn't much past, for the five o'clock post hadn't come in, nor much before, for I come on duty at five after my tea, and I had just got back."

"The manager was talking to you when the message came, I understand?"

"Was he? Possibly. I don't remember."

"You think he wasn't?"

"I *thought* he came up after the post got in. But, of course, I may be wrong. One day's so like another."

"But I understand that he, too, heard the 'phone?"

"He might have done that—the 'phone is to one side of the desk—but I didn't see him."

"Did Mr. Eames give any reason as to why he was determined to have one of the first floor rooms looking into the street?"

"None whatever."

"Were the rooms you offered him instead as good?"

"One was better."

"Has he ever stayed in the hotel before?"

"No."

"Sure?"

"Quite. I came here when the hotel opened."

"Isn't there a balcony running all along your front rooms on the first floor, and also along the rooms of the Marvel Hotel next door?"

"Yes. Both hotels belong to the same management."

The Chief Inspector seemed plunged in thought for a moment. "By the way, before I forget it, from which direction did the manager come when he spoke to you after Eames' 'phone had been taken? I want to get the whole scene clear in my mind."

"From the direction of the stairs."

"And now about the voice over the 'phone—it wasn't Eames himself, you think?"

"Sure it wasn't. This sounded like an old chap with a cold in his head."

"Wheezy?"

"More than that. Funniest voice—sort of muffled—I should know it again anywhere."

"A disguised voice," wrote the Chief Inspector.

"Had Eames any friends?"

"Never saw him speak to a soul."

"Did any letters come for him?"

"Not a card."

"How would you say that, generally speaking, he spent his time in the hotel?"

"Smoking cigarettes in the lounge. Of course we've had rotten weather, but I don't think Mr. Eames was out of the house for more than ten minutes at a stretch."

"Did he go out often?"

"Always after each meal. Acted as though he intended to live to be a hundred. And to think that all the time he meant to commit suicide! Why, he might have had any kind of a bust-up." The booking-clerk evidently considered that Eames had wasted a rare chance.

"Now about Mr. Beale's arrival?"

But there the booking-clerk could tell the Chief Inspector nothing fresh.

"And now I want to know what luggage, however small, left the hotel after mid-day to-day. I'm afraid I'll have to have the day-porter routed out, too."

"I can tell you from the books that there were no departures to-day after twelve o'clock. As a matter of fact, not a bag left the hotel after a quarter-past eleven. It's one of our strictest rules that nothing leaves a room without first 'phoning down to the clerk to find out if it's all O.K."

"But what about the people in the hotel taking out

their bags themselves?"

"Oh, that,—of course—but not this afternoon." The clerk thought back, "You see it's a small hotel, and I'm paid to keep my eyes open. Nobody took out any bag bigger than a woman's wrist-bag after one o'clock. There's no business doing of a Saturday afternoon. The day-porter's gone home and won't be visible till Monday."

"What about when you're off duty, Mr. Page?"

"The manager relieves me for two hours at noon, from one to three, but as the dining-room opens out of the hall, and my table is just by the glass door, I'm as good as in the hall. At seven o'clock the hall-porter takes my place till seven-thirty. But, as I say, I've my eyes on the hall all the time, and if there's any crush I'm out in two twos."

The clerk yawned dismally, and Pointer, with a laugh, let him go, after having him write down the names of any of the occupants of the five balcony rooms which were not known to the management from other visits. There were only two. Numbers eleven and twelve; and of these, number eleven was "expecting to leave" daily.

"Now, who do I see about the service-stairs—who is supposed to keep an eye on them?"

"The housekeeper. She's still up; I'll send her to you."

The housekeeper assured him that at noon by Saturday the service-door just beyond the manager's suite was duly locked and bolted. After that hour it could only be used with her consent and approval. The lower door in the basement—the delivery door proper—was, of course, another matter. The key of the upper door hung in the maids' sitting-room just opposite,—a small room used especially by the maid who waited on the manager.

"That door leads to the maids' sitting-room and to the service-stairs, doesn't it?"

The Chief Inspector pointed to a door opening out of the manager's little lobby. He opened it as he spoke —not for the first time that night.

The housekeeper looked surprised. "Bless me, sir, it doesn't take you police gentlemen long to find your way about."

"And that is the door leading into the street, eh?"

"Yes, sir."

"It's not locked now."

"Oh, yes, it is, sir." She laid a confident hand on it to turn in bewilderment as it opened easily.

"Why—why—someone must have undone it!"

"Just so," agreed Pointer dryly. "And the key?"

She opened a door facing the street entrance, and switched on the light. "There it is, hanging where I put it at twelve o'clock."

Pointer raised a weary eyebrow, but he said nothing, and made his way to the lounge, where, after asking both the manager and Mr. Beale to hold themselves in readiness for any possible further questions tomorrow morning, he joined Watts upstairs and spent a strenuous hour with him.

"No key to fit his trunk—no sign of the bag which the booking-clerk and porter saw him carry upstairs,—no sign of a ring,—no scrap of paper nor any mark of identity beyond his signatures,—humph!"

The Chief Inspector dusted his knees carefully and went to the mantelpiece. "Here's a box of wax vestas right enough, the same kind as the vesta I picked up in the wardrobe, but that one was still warm and soft. Burnt down to the last end and dropped burning into the wardrobe when it scorched someone's fingers—whose, Watts?"

Watts shook his head.

"—Not more than half-an-hour before we came into the room, so Eames couldn't have done it, for more reasons than one."

"I saw you try the electric torch in that American gent.'s bag, sir," Watts threw in.

"Just so. It was out of order. He didn't say a word about that in his evidence downstairs. You noticed those marks on the top of the wardrobe, where someone had evidently passed a stiff brush over it, presumably to do away with any finger marks or streaks?"

"I did, sir. And wasn't his—I mean Mr. Beale's—clothes-brush in a fearful state. He did look put out when you picked it up first thing."

The Chief Inspector nodded with a grim smile. "Aye, he did. He might have thought it less of a give-away if he'd known that all along he had a fine smear of dust on the under part of his sleeve. A smear that could only have been got up there. The manager's coat was clean, though that proves little. I hope you noticed the washstand before the doctor washed his hands?"

Watts was an honest young fellow, and he flushed by way of answer.

"The towel was damp, so was the soap. So was the inside of the basin. The jug was half empty, but there wasn't a drop of water in the pail. Whatever water had been used had been flung out of the window. It's been pouring so hard all day that a bit more or less would never be noticed. But the fact is odd. Why should anyone mind pouring the basin into the pail?"

"The water was too black after that wardrobe top," laughed Watts. The Chief Inspector was popular with his men, and Watts was, moreover, a distant connection.

"Then that chest of drawers. You know the feeling of using a key after a pass-key?"

"As though the lock were stuck, sir?"

"Just so. I turned the key very slowly, and each 'drawer had been last opened with a pass-key, or rather locked with one. And that smell of tobacco when we opened them—same smell as Mr. Beale's cigars. And that dusting of cigar ash on one of the ties. I shouldn't wonder if this is going to turn into a very funny case, Watts. I shouldn't wonder at all."

Watts' eyes brightened. A "funny case" from the point of view of the police often leads to promotion, and though Pointer was the youngest Chief Inspector at the Yard, Watts believed he could unravel any tangle.

Pointer lived in Bayswater. He liked its open squares and clearer air. He shared three rooms there with a friend, James O'Connor, now a bookbinder, but during the War a very successful member of the Secret Service. Talkative, gossipy, and secretive was the Celt. Only a few had any idea of the hard core of blue steel that lay beneath his apparent easy-going cheeriness. Pointer was one of these few. He and O'Connor had worked once together, the one openly representing the law, the other secretly endangering his life every moment of the day while tracking down a German-American-Irish plot. O'Connor never referred to those days, though, had his means permitted, he would have liked to continue his hazardous work; but with peace he had to turn his attention to making a livelihood, and being single-minded in all his doings, he refused absolutely to be drawn into any of his friend's problems except as the merest onlooker.

It always gave the Chief Inspector genuine pleasure to step from the little lobby into the huge living-room which the two men used in common. He saw richer rooms often, but never one which suited him so well, with its ivory walls and paint, kept up to the mark by his own neat brush, the thick, short, draw-curtains of apple-green silk to the four windows, the chair covers of a Persian pattern—green leaves rioting over a cream ground, with here and there a pomegranate or a blue bird—book cases in quiet walnut stood against the walls Pointer's large writing desk, and O'Connor's equally huge table, filled the corners by the windows. In one open fireplace logs were heaped, the other was kept free for burning papers. The soft brightness of his home was like a friendly hand clasp to the weary police officer after the rain outside.

O'Connor smiled up at him and pointed to the table.

"Mrs. Able is thirsting for your blood. I told her to leave the things the last time she brought them in. I couldn't face her again." He turned out an electric hot-plate as he spoke.

A vegetable soup, a dish of Tatar *bitokes*—savoury balls of beefsteak and marrow and seasonings pounded to perfection and browned to a turn, a well-made potato salad, some crisp rolls, and a glass of light wine made Pointer ready for another stretch of work if need be.

When the meal was cleared away by his landlady, who ruled the two men with her cooking, he filled his pipe from a beautiful covered jar of modern Japanese enamel where gold fish glittered among green waves. Jim's tobacco lived in a dull blue pot at the other end, and in the middle stood the room's one useless ornament, a carved Chinese ball-puzzle, fine as a birch leaf and showing ball within ball in tantalising glimpses of colour. It typified his calling to the policeman. He picked it up again and turned it gently to and fro.

"Yes," he said ruminatingly, "get hold of your key and you'll open up all right. But how to get hold of your key—"

"I thought the Meredith case was practically over," murmured O'Connor through clouds of smoke.

"Finished at eight. I've another case on now, and rather a stiff one, or all signs belie it. It's a hotel case, and you know how I feel about them."

"Still, old chap, you did very well with that robbery down at Ramsgate. It gave you your leg-up."

There was nothing Pointer enjoyed more than talking his cases over with his friend, whose discretion was as much to be trusted as his own. Not that he often got an opinion out of the Irishman, but the mere reciting aloud of the various phases of a problem in itself helped to clear his mind.

"They are the very devil all the same. You never know where you are. Take a private house—and the servants, the furniture, the rooms, the very walls can give you points, but a hotel! How can you follow up a hundred or so possible criminals? Personally, if I ever go in for a murder I should never dream of choosing any other place."

"A murder case, eh?"

"Did I say so? Well, see what you think. This is how things stand at present."

He told of his call to the Enterprise and the results of the inquiry so far.

"Why don't you think it's a suicide, what's wrong with that letter?" Jim handed it back. "You say the writing is the same as on the register."

"By the same hand you'd think, but this letter's been written with an ordinary pen, same nib and ink as is supplied in the hotel bedroom, yet Eames had a filled fountain-pen in his pocket. He signed the register with it, why didn't he use it to write this letter with? It wasn't as if he had been trying to disguise his handwriting. Then the way he was huddled into the wardrobe looked as if his feet had been shoved in first and the rest of his body afterwards. You'll see what I mean when I show you Lester's photos on Monday. His coat and tie were half over his head at the back. And where is his trunk key? You might say that he got rid of his bag beforehand to save tracing his home, but he left the trunk. Then why not leave the key? And the things he had put into the wardrobe from his bed and washstand—pyjamas, shaving-tackle, and that sort of thing —well, of course a man *might* lock himself into a pitch-dark wardrobe and then proceed to tidy all the articles neatly against the front, but it's difficult to see why."

"Especially if he was drugged. Sure it wasn't an overdose of whisky? That would explain so many puzzles." O'Connor loved to impersonate guileless curiosity at these talks. It moved the Chief Inspector to a fury at times which the Irishman took as a tribute to his histrionic powers.

"Any finger prints?" he asked after a moment.

It was Pointer's turn to get even. He gazed on his friend as on a man past praying for. "Any finger-prints? How many things were there, do you suppose, that that American and the Manager between them hadn't pawed over? There was a regular finger-mark jam over everything. Now I'll tell you another thing. His socks and small things were in the two top-drawers. Nothing could have been tidier. Even his spare shoelaces had rubber bands to keep them trim. His underwear, in the top long drawer, looked as if it were ready for an inspection, but his things in the bottom drawer —two pairs of trousers and a coat—seemed as though they had been flung in during an earthquake."

"Inference—someone was chiefly concerned in pockets." Jim was so interested that he forgot his role.

"Aye, just so. His trunk was in the same muddle. And remember, no letters, no papers!"

"You said his trunk and underwear were all oldish and all marked R.E.?"

"They are."

There was silence for some time in the room. Then:

"I shall put a personal in all Monday's papers offering a reward of three pounds for any information concerning his watch. Thank Heaven, watches have numbers. That may lead us somewhere. Eames' clothes have a Colonial look to me, and his umbrella has a Toronto mark on it, but as far as I can see, the watch is our best chance to find out who he really is, and where he comes from. He entered himself as a dentist, but that pencil in his pocket was sharpened either by an artist or a draughtsman of some kind."

"What about the American?"

"Aye, what about him? And what about the manager, too?"

"The manager? You think he shares your opinion as to the advantages of a hotel for—let us call it working off old scores?"

"I stopped on my way home to look up his record," Pointer continued unmoved; "it's his first job of the kind. But his father was manager of the Metropole at Scarborough. There's nothing against his character so far."

"Ah, just let him wait till you have another go at him."

"The Enterprise has always been a well conducted house under him."

"Say no more," begged O'Connor, "his guilt seems piling up with every second."

"I hope to trace that 'phone call on Monday."

"Disguised voice making you think of the manager? Sherlock Holmes putting two and two together after having looked at the answer in the back of the book." O'Connor laid down his tool to strike an attitude.

"The manager might have sent it, that's my only point so far."

"And what about the American, the one you have your eye on because you think he threw his wash-water out of the window? What else have you ag'in him?"

"He recognised Eames. Or at least he knows something about him, about his death possibly. I'll bet you anything you like I'm not mistaken. His control over his face is what you'd expect from a big newspaper' man, but just for a second, when he thought no one was watching, he looked down at Eames' face with— well, there was recognition of some kind in his eye, and a lot besides—a lot! I had my small looking-glass in my hand under my handkerchief and was studying him."

"The Embassy seems a good reference. Perhaps he was bluffing when he gave it you?"

Pointer shook his head. "I don't think so. Mr. Beale is a somebody all right, or I'm much mistaken."

"You certainly ought to know the genuine article. You see enough of the imitation. And now I suppose some downtrodden underling of yours is keeping a skinned orb upon both these desperate criminals?" Jim got up and stretched himself.

"They are that!" responded the other fervently.

"Alf!" called O'Connor a little later from his opened bedroom door.

"Well?" came in a muffled voice.

"If it was Beale who searched those drawers why that jumbled haste? Sure he didn't need to fetch the manager till he was ready? Same brainwave applies to the manager and yourself."

Pointer made no reply.

"Another thought. If Eames committed suicide why fasten himself up in a hotel wardrobe. Why not choose a bench in the park?" persisted the seeker after enlightenment.

The banging of the door between the two rooms was the only reply.

CHAPTER TWO

Pointer liked to be up with the lark though he spent his time somewhat differently. It was barely six o'clock next morning when he took himself to the Marvel Hotel.

"Look here, Gay"—the Detective Inspector was well-known to the booking-clerk, who had a brother at the Yard—"strictly between ourselves, there's some trouble in a balcony room next door. Something's missing. Who have you got in your rooms that open on to the same balcony?"

The clerk ran a finger up his register.

"Number two left early this morning, the rest are still abed I take it."

Pointer swung the book around. Number two was registered to a James Cox of Birmingham. Profession — Medical student.

"At what hour did he leave?"

"About four."

"Room empty?" asked the other quickly. "Good, I'll go up and have a look at it." Reaching for the key, he was half-way up the stairs before the clerk had finished his nod.

Pointer found the room still untouched by the chamber-maid, and he locked the door behind him with an air of relief. The bed had not been slept in. On the corner of the table lay a wax vesta, the counterpart of the ones already reposing in the Detective Inspector's black bag.

The linoleum in front of the French window showed where muddy boots had walked up and down. Both the length of the stride and the size of the marks spoke for a tall man. On the balcony outside, the rain had washed away all chance of tracks on the stone, but on the waist-high grating, which was all that separated the rooms of the Marvel from those of the Enterprise, were a few small mud-clots close in by the wall, and under the shelter of the iron roof. Room number fourteen was nearest to the Marvel, and in front of its window even the rain had not been able to remove all traces of the muddy feet which had apparently stood first on one side and then on the other, as though a man had been trying to peer in through the blind.

Looking in, Pointer saw Watts talking to Miller, who had been left on duty in the room all night. Yet even so, those tracks on the balcony could not have been made many hours before the rain stopped. Someone had walked from one window to the other after he and Watts had left the place.

He tapped on the pane, and Watts joined him outside. He had already seen the marks.

"And look there, sir," he pointed to a sodden heap of canvas, apparently an awning, which, judging by its appearance, must have lain for months between the windows of number fourteen and number twelve of the Enterprise. There were a couple of deep indentations on it, one beside the other. Pointer took out the sheet of tracings he had made yesterday at the door leading out into the street from the service-stairs. He and Watts tried them carefully. They could have been made by the same feet.

"Smallish feet. They just fit Miller, sir, as I was pointing out to him when you tapped," observed Watts facetiously, and the two Scotland Yard men stepped into the room where Miller was waiting to make his report. He had been dozing in the easy chair when he had heard a couple of light taps on the pane. Very carefully he had pushed the blind aside and looked out. Instantly a torch was flashed in his eyes, blinding him. When he got the window open, no one was to be seen.

"Of course, I couldn't hear anything, sir. You know what the wind was like, though the rain had pretty fair stopped by them. It was exactly twenty minutes past three o'clock."

"Did you get any idea of who held the torch?"

"Only that he was a big chap, sir. Big as you."

"Did you see anyone on the opposite side of the window?"

"No, sir."

"Could you have seen anyone there?"

The detective was positive that he could and would, as he had looked up and down the balcony, which was fairly well lit by the street lights. He had not tried to investigate further, as his orders had been not to leave the room.

On the balcony outside, the Chief Inspector stood for a second by the heap of canvas. "Just run the blind down inside there, and turn on the light."

After a moment Pointer tapped, as a signal that the window was to be opened again. "You can see better into the room from the other side—the side nearest the Marvel."

"You think it was someone from the Enterprise, sir, who wanted to be sure of getting back unnoticed?"

"Looks that way."

"You don't think that two men could have been out there together, sir?"

Pointer did not reply as he stepped into the room again, and sent Miller off for breakfast and sleep.

"Now, about that morphia taken. Of course we shall know for certain in the morning, but I take it that there's no doubt but that it was morphia all right. It's an odd thing that we couldn't find any cup or glass from which the stuff was drunk. From what the doctor said as to the amount, it's not likely that Eames could have washed up after his drink, nor can I see the point. Let's have another hunt."

And they did, with no better result.

"Could he have flung the glass over the balcony railing?" Watts measured the distance carefully. "Yes, a man could, fairly easily."

"After a heavy drug?" Pointer's voice was sceptical. "And what about passers-by?" He picked up a bottle from the wash-stand labelled "The Cough Mixture." It bore the name of a near-by chemist.

"I tasted that last night, sir. It's some I often take myself. It hasn't been tampered with in any way." Watts' tone was as good as a respectful hint not to waste time in a blind alley.

Pointer scrutinised the bottle through his glass, and finally wrapped it up with special care, putting it in his black bag. He told Watts of the match which he had found in room two of the Marvel next door. Evidently Mr. Cox of Birmingham used the identical kind,—which was odd considering its foreign origin,—favoured by someone in room fourteen of the Enterprise.

"Mr. Beale spoke of having just come from France, didn't he, sir?"

"He did."

"He may have forgotten that he had left his matches on the mantelpiece after lighting one to see into the wardrobe. Perhaps it was he who left the match you found in the Marvel. Anyone could get over that tiny railing between the two hotels."

"Quite possible," and Pointer wrapped the box, too, carefully up again, and locked his bag.

His next move was to interview the clerk of the Marvel as to the appearance and general behaviour of Mr. Cox.

He learnt but little. Mr. Cox had arrived very late on Saturday night in a little two-seater which proclaimed itself as hired at a glance. He seemed a very quiet, unobtrusive young man, carried his own bag, and had barely attracted one glance from the booking-clerk, who only gleaned a general idea of a big young fellow with a pronounced limp, in a grey tweed suit and soft grey hat. He had driven his car away without asking any directions or making any inquiries as to a garage, and had returned shortly on foot. This would have been about one o'clock. His room had been waiting for him for nearly a week. On July 30th a 'phone call had asked whether any of the balcony rooms were free. There were two vacancies. The voice asked the numbers. They were two and seven. Number two was chosen, and the hotel was asked to keep the room for a Mr. Cox who would be there within the hour. This was about eleven o'clock in the morning. Half an hour later a messenger boy brought a letter for the manager, who passed it over to the book-keeper. In it Mr. Cox stated that he might be unable to occupy the room immediately, but wished No. 2 reserved for him. He enclosed four one-pound notes as a deposit. The Chief Inspector annexed the letter. When Mr. Cox finally arrived on Saturday, August 3rd, the room was still his, and when about four a.m. he descended, still with his bag, and walked out of the front door without saying a word, the hotel expected him to return for some sort of a belated breakfast. Up to the present hour he had not been seen again, but the day was still very young, as the clerk pointed out.

"Did you see in what direction he went?"

But nobody had taken sufficient interest to watch.

Pointer pulled out a print of Eames' dead face.

"Before July 30th—before that room was 'phoned for —did this man ask for a room here?"

The clerk recognised the face at once. "Yes, about an hour or two before Cox's 'phone came. Seemed a nice, friendly sort of chap. Now I come to think of it, he, too, asked for a balcony room, and went up to have a look at two and seven. He didn't take either; I forget why."

"Did the 'phone message you got later sound at all like his voice?"

But that the clerk couldn't remember. "Now I come to think of it, it didn't sound like Cox speaking. Cox talked like a Colonial,—the few words he spoke asking about his room, and saying that he had 'phoned for one on July 30th and sent a letter with a deposit"

"You didn't tell me that before, Gay: that's an important point. I want to get hold of Cox if I can. Want to ask him a few questions."

"Well, Mr. Chief Inspector, a chap can't think of everything at once," responded the clerk good-humouredly; with which view of the limitations of the human intellect Pointer agreed.

He arranged that a call should be sent through at once if the young man returned to the hotel, and left feeling that he had found out quite sufficient to pay him for his early Sunday morning. Eames had been in to prospect for his friend—or his enemy, whichever Cox was—not long after he had taken a room at the Enterprise for himself. The letter signed "Cox" was very unlike that man's signature in the register, but very like the letter left in Eames' pocket for the manager; and whatever Pointer's doubts about it, he did not attempt to deny to himself that the writing in that letter exactly resembled Eames' entry on the hotel book, though perhaps, to his keen eyes, a trifle laboured-looking. It would be a nice little problem for the handwriting expert, but, to his thinking, there was an ease and a freedom about this last letter—the one sent in Cox's name—which suggested a genuine document. Had he been able to get a fair description of the man, he would have sent Cox's description to every station in England, for he did not share the hotel's belief in his return, but, bar his size and the limp, which were the easiest of disguises, he had no definite idea as to the man's appearance.

He glanced at his watch. Nine o'clock. Time to see if the manager and Mr. Beale had remembered any fresh details. The manager was at his breakfast, and Pointer thought that his manner had changed in some subtle way from what it had been last night. Mr. Beale was apparently not up yet. As Pointer particularly wished to question him, he sent the hotel's one and only page to the room which had been assigned to the American for the rest of the night—it happened to be the manager's sitting-room—with a polite message as to the pleasure it would give the Chief Inspector to be allowed a few minutes' conversation in room No. 14.

The boy came back with bulging eyes.

"I believe the gentleman's killed hisself too, sir," he hissed melodramatically in Pointer's ear. Evidently the news about No. 14 had leaked out among the staff.

For once the Scotland Yard man acted like any mere mortal, and bounded from his chair. "What?"

"Well, there ain't no sound, and I can't make him answer, though I've hammered and banged like anything on his door." The boy was evidently thoroughly enjoying himself.

"Idiot! Keep your mouth shut! Ask the manager to come here a moment," was the somewhat contradictory directions he received in a tone which made Pointer's meaning clear.

The manager arrived, a trifle breathless, and the two men entered the lobby into which both his bedroom and his sitting-room opened. They tried the sitting- room door. It was locked, and no reply came from within to voice or knock.

"There's a door into it from my bedroom. I have the key, and the bolt's on the bedroom side." The manager, who was very white, led the way, and after a second's wait unlocked the door and flung it open. A burst of fresh air met them. The window stood ajar. The room was empty. The other door locked and bolted. A bag, half-open, stood at the foot of the bed which had been made up on the couch, and which had evidently not been slept in. A half-burnt cigar lay on the carpet by the armchair, together with a novel. The electric lamp was still on. Pointer felt the end of the cigar.

"Been out some time. Excuse me, sir, you're standing on a piece of paper."

The manager jumped away as though his companion had spoken of a live coal. Pointer carelessly ran the little wisp of green and white striped paper through his fingers as he looked at the sill, and out on the pavement, which was on a level with the floor. Provided there was the will, there certainly was an easy enough way. But why the will? Why should the editor of an important newspaper leave by the window rather than by the door, even though he were an American?

He looked Mr. Beale's bag over. Nothing had been taken. He saw in it no paper to match the little end he had "absent-mindedly" stuffed into his pocket.

"I thought I saw a piece of striped paper lying around" —he glanced about him—"did it belong to anything of yours?"

The manager shook his head. He was even paler than he had been.

"Was it anything of yours, sir?" persisted the officer, peering under the table.

"No." The manager's voice was harsh.

"Odd sort of paper, too. Oh, here it is"—Pointer fished it out, "Did you see anything like it in Mr. Beale's hands last night?"

"I suppose on a modest estimate I had near a dozen people in this room yesterday." The manager's voice was studiously level. "I should say that the probabilities are that any one of them dropped that little tag."

"Shouldn't wonder," agreed Pointer amicably. "Did you and Mr. Beale sit up long together last night?"

The manager hesitated for the fraction of a second. "N—no, not beyond saying good-night, after his refusing to let me give him my bedroom."

"You didn't discuss Mr. Eames?"

"Not at all. Not at all."

"Kindly look carefully around the room and see if anything is missing."

The manager obeyed, and Pointer with one deft swoop, while he back was turned, emptied the contents of an ash-tray, which stood on a little table between two easy chairs, into an envelope. Then he sauntered casually into the bedroom, and watched the manager in a mirror, as he aimlessly took up trifle after trifle, stopping now and then to stare out of the window with a puzzled, worried look. Suddenly he seemed to leave the world of speculations.

"I say, Inspector, this is all rot! Mr. Beale isn't a thief. You saw his passport, and I saw a letter of credit and various other letters of his."

"Have you any idea, sir, as to when he left this room?"

"I dozed off about three o'clock. Last night's affair doesn't help a manager to sleep any better than usual, you know. So I suppose Mr. Beale must have left some time after that?"

"You had no idea why he left by the window?"

"I? Certainly not! I know no more than you do about the whole affair. Probably not so much," he added with a rather forced smile.

Pointer went carefully all over the little suite of three rooms, with its lobby opening into the lounge and on to the landing of the service-stairs with a door into the street. He found nothing to detain him, and rapidly drafted a notice to be sent out to all taxi-drivers describing Mr. Beale, and asking for news of any fare resembling him picked up on Sunday morning or late Saturday night. Watts was off duty, with his family at the Zoo, but the Chief Inspector had no time for relaxation.

He sent Miller to find out which maid was responsible for the manager's rooms and to send her up at once. Miller, who had made himself quite popular in the staff breakfast-room, slipped away, and within ten minutes ushered in a very fluttered young woman.

"Now, my dear, did you make up a bed in the manager's sitting-room late last night?"

"Oh, no, sir. I was in bed when it all happened. Oh, dear no, sir." And she edged towards the door.

"Come, come, I don't bite, you know. Then did you do up his room this morning?"

That was better. Kate twitteringly acknowledged that she had.

"Did you see anything of a letter I left on the bedroom table? The window was open at the top, it may have blown on to the floor; anyway, I haven't been able to find it."

The maid had seen nothing of any paper, which was not surprising, as Pointer had just invented it. "Besides, sir, the manager would have been sure to see it. He didn't go to bed at all, nor even lie down."

"Tut! Tut! Worried, I suppose, by all the bother. He generally sleeps so well, too."

He had learnt what he wanted to know, and the girl was allowed to scuttle away from his terrifying presence.

Pointer next made his way to a window on the first floor landing. It, too, looked on to the balcony. He examined the sill with his magnifying glass very carefully, and bending out scrutinised the boards below.

"Come here, Miller," he called softly, "could you scramble out of that window?"

The detective proved that he could, provided that he were helped, but he found it difficult.

"When the manager, and that American gentleman, left No. 14 last night, did you see them go on down the stairs?"

"I saw them turn on to this landing, sir, but I couldn't see this window from where I was. I thought I heard their footsteps go on down."

"The wind was rather rough. One or both might have come up quietly again and got out."

"I don't think anyone could have opened that window without my hearing them. And I think I should have felt the draught, sir."

"Humph!" was all Pointer said to himself, as he walked on out of the hotel and took a train to Streatham where lived Doctor Burden, the great Government analyst, expert in poisons, and reasons for sudden deaths.

Pointer had barely pushed open the gate of the drive when the doctor met him, swinging along, golf sticks under his arm. Too late he tried to dodge behind a clump of laurels, the law was upon him.

"Just a moment, doctor. It's only for a second, sir," begged the police officer, with a firm grip on the clubs. "It really won't take you more than one glance. All I want to know is whether a spot on a label is morphia solution or not. That's all."

"I know you, Pointer." The doctor tried to wrest his irons free; "you got me last time with that yarn, and tied me up in a thirty-six hour job before I knew where I was. Never again!"

"But this time it really is only one spot of what I think may be a solution of morphia that I'm after."

He won, and the doctor, growling at his folly in having gone to Service instead of straight on to the links, led him into his study.

Pointer unpacked the bottle of cough-mixture which he had taken from the washstand in No. 14.

"Here, sir, where the writing has run a bit on the label. Could that smear be morphia? The stuff in the bottle is all right, I fancy, but it'll be sent to you tomorrow to test at your leisure."

"Leisure!" groaned the analyst, "you're a wag. My leisure!" He took the bottle and disappeared through a door to return in a couple of minutes. "It is morphia. And in a solution strong enough to kill an elephant. Don't ask me for exact quantities, I'm off."

"Very much obliged to you, sir," grinned the Chief Inspector, as he carefully replaced the bottle, and followed the doctor at a more leisurely pace out of the garden.

"The case begins to move at last," he murmured to himself with satisfaction. He proceeded to jog along still further by ringing the private bell of Mr. Redman, the chemist, until that gentleman opened the door.

At the sight of the officer, whom he knew, his face softened a little from its "disturbed-at-Sunday-dinner" severity.

"Anything I can do for you, officer?" He waved him

into the passage.

"It's just this, Mr. Redman," this time the print of young Eames was produced. "Do you remember selling anything to this gentleman any day last week, or say since about July 25th?"

The chemist shook his head.

"But my assistant hasn't gone home yet; he dines with us on Sundays, we keep the shop open till twelve, you know—I'll call him."

The assistant looked curiously at the snapshot.

"What did he die of?"

"Suicide. Inquest isn't till Tuesday or Wednesday," parried Pointer. "Do you recognise him? Ever sold anything to him this last week or even yesterday?"

The assistant shook his head.

"Never saw him before."

"Quite sure?" Pointer had not expected this.

"Oh, absolutely."

"Humph. Well, what about this bottle? It was standing on the dead man's washstand." He produced the cough mixture.

The two men agreed that the bottle came from them.

"Could you call to mind any people you sold one like it to? It's a very important point in the case."

"But there's nothing whatever in that medicine," began the two chemists hastily, and perhaps more truthfully than they intended.

"I know there isn't. That's not the point. The point is who bought this bottle?"

"Let me see," Mr. Redman rubbed his nose reflectively with his glasses. We don't sell much of that at this season of the year. Yesterday's crop of colds hasn't had time to mature yet—now let me see, a woman bought a bottle on Friday, but it was the two shilling size."

"I sold a bottle like that early in the week," the assistant spoke with certainty, "to a tall young fellow, an American he struck me as being. Said he wanted it for a chum of his who had a bad cold. I remember now! It was"—he paused—"I know! It was Tuesday just as I was shutting up— Seven o'clock that would be, or say three minutes past."

"Could you describe him?"

The assistant could; and except for the fact that the man limped badly, the description might have fitted thousands of young men. Incidentally, however, it fitted Mr. Cox of the Marvel Hotel to a nicety. "Tall, broad-shouldered, in a rather crumpled tweed suit, and felt hat, clean-shaven, dark hair, dark brown eyes, and a square jaw. I'll bet he served during the war."

Neither the chemist nor his assistant had made up any morphia for over a month. A glance at their poison-book confirmed this.

So last Tuesday evening—on July 30th, to be exact — Mr. Cox had purchased the bottle of medicine for Mr. Eames—the same Mr. Eames who on that same Tuesday, but in the morning, had inspected a room which had later been taken by a letter which Pointer believed to have been written by Eames, though signed in the name of Cox—. The officer turned these tangled facts over in his mind as he smoked a pipe in the Enterprise lounge. Was Cox a friend or an enemy? If he was the criminal, why had he returned last night? Had he left some clue behind him which he must recover at all costs? Or had he been disturbed by some sound in the afternoon, and returned— unconscious that the dead man had already been discovered—to complete his work? In this case, what had he left undone?

At any rate, Watts would have a vague description to go on to-morrow in his hunt for a possible purchaser of morphia.

Pointer spent the rest of the afternoon apparently gossiping with all and sundry. Each conversation, however, resembled all others in that, though it might begin with the weather or cricket, it invariably finished up with the manager's whereabouts yesterday afternoon.

He had been seen about half-past three, and he had

been seen just after five, but in the intervals it seemed impossible to locate him exactly. Pointer wished heartily that Eames' death had occurred at midnight. It would have made no difference to Eames but a great deal to the detectives.

Of Eames himself he learnt but little. The young man had apparently made no clear impression on those with whom he had come in contact, save that they all ascribed to him unusual powers of silence.

The maid had nothing to report beyond that "the gentleman of No. 14 left his room always at eight o'clock regular." A couple of books lay always on his table—not novels—thick, "solid-looking books. Pointer showed her two,—"yes, those were the very identical ones." They were works on dentistry, very new and unused, with "Reginald Eames" neatly written in each. To Pointer they did not look as though their late owner had spent much time poring over them. The maid went on to say that any remarks of hers had been met with a brevity she evidently considered amounted to silence.

"Don't think he knew how to open his mouth, but there, what with meaning to take his life it's no wonder, —what I mean to say, you couldn't expect him to go on like an ordinary young man, could you?"

Pointer agreed that to a woman of her keen perceptions a difference might be discernible. Had she ever seen any letters lying around?

"Not lying about, no; but she had twice seen Mr. Eames standing by the window reading letters. No, they hadn't looked like old ones—in fact, once she had seen him opening the envelope. On each occasion it had been shortly after breakfast, when she had brought in a carafe left to be cleaned with the others on the floor. Each time Eames had looked around as though not relishing the interruption. He certainly was that sunk in his letters, though it was only a couple of those large square sheets. What I mean to say, not real letters,—*you* know."

The last time she had heard him lock the bedroom

door after her had been on Saturday morning. Yes, she was quite sure that it was yesterday, because directly she heard of the suicide she had thought of that letter. The time before might have been a Wednesday or Thursday—she couldn't be sure.

"Had he looked worried when she saw him?"

No, only awfully keen, and eager, and though he wasn't smiling exactly, he had looked distinctly pleased —this was on Saturday. She had heard him whistling later on as she swept next door.

"Were the sheets typed or written?"

"Written in very close, tiny lines."

Pointer showed her Cox's letter to the Marvel about his room. She was certain that the writing had been much smaller, and also that the paper was different. She had had to come quite close to put the carafe on the table—"Trust you for that," agreed Pointer mentally— and had not been able to help seeing the writing, and the paper all in tiny squares.

"Eh?"

"The paper, sir, all ruled in little squares—such funny paper!" She was quite sure that she had never seen anything of a striped green and white shiny paper such as the detective now showed her.

"Not at any time, sir."

Questioned as to the exact hour when she had last seen Eames yesterday morning, she put it down at about eleven o'clock—the occasion which she had just been telling about when she had seen the young man busy with his letter.

About the afternoon she could say nothing, as on Saturdays she helped in the ironing room from three to six o'clock.

As to visitors, she knew of none. She never saw anyone entering or leaving No. 14 but Mr. Eames himself. No, she had never heard any voices in the room. Asked about a bag, she had seen one once on the table when Mr. Eames was in the room, but never but the once. He kept his wardrobe locked, and she had imagined the bag to be inside. It was yesterday morning when she had seen it for the first and only time. As to his door, he always kept that unlocked,—"I mean to say, unless he was dressing or undressing."

"Now, about Mr. Beale—the gentleman who had occupied No. 14 that evening, had she ever seen him before?"

"Well, sir, I thought I had yesterday morning coming along the corridor with the manager, but the house-keeper said it was quite another gentleman, a Mr. Sikes she called him, but he certainly did look very like the American gentleman, as I said to him myself."

"Said to whom?"

"To the gentleman last night when I made up the room. He was sitting by the window, and I said to him that surely I had seen him earlier in the day— what I mean to say"

"What did Mr. Beale say?" asked Pointer, feeling that flesh and blood could stand but little more of this damsel's conversation.

She could not remember what reply her remark had called forth, which was not surprising, since Mr. Beale, as a matter of fact, had received it in silence.

He could learn nothing more from her except that the hour when she had met the man whom she took to be Mr. Beale in company with the manager, had been sometime during the lunch hour,—between one and two-thirty, in other words. All his skill in bringing the conversation around to the manager brought him no reward. She knew nothing of anyone's movements yesterday afternoon, so with a compliment on her clear way of stating facts she was dismissed.

Alone in the room, Pointer unlocked one of the two top drawers whose tidiness had struck him last night. He put his hand to the back and brought out a little box wrapped neatly in green and white striped paper. He compared it with the torn end which he had picked up in the manager's sitting-room. It was identical. The square in which a small box of pearl studs was folded was entire. It must have been from another piece this corner came. Had it also been wrapped around jewellery? He looked at the studs. They were small but good ones. Genuine as far as he could tell— at any rate the gold stems and general workmanship looked like a superior article. He took the little box from the drawer and promoted it to a resting place in his black bag, to be transferred on the morrow to his safe at the Yard. The piece of paper the manager had stepped on so promptly he put into an envelope beside it.

CHAPTER THREE

Pointer had been certain from the first that Eames must have had some place not far from the hotel to which his correspondence was directed. Moreover, early that morning he had marked a small tobacconist in a poor street around the corner, quite out of the run of usual passers-by, as the most likely nook to which Eames would have had his letters sent. Since then he had learnt more. The paper, ruled in little squares— suggesting a foreign origin—the small, close writing like that used by Cox in the hotel register next door; Eames' eager interest on the last morning he had been alive, his whistling later in the same day, were all additional material for the mosaic the police had to fit together. Downstairs Pointer learnt that the only Mr. Sikes known to the hotel had been there a few times, but had never been seen to come in merely as a visitor. Neither the clerk nor the hall porter remembered seeing him yesterday. But as that had been an unusually strenuous time of welcoming coming and speeding parting guests, Mr. Sikes might have passed unnoticed, though both men thought this most unlikely. He certainly had not made himself known in any way.

On the register he was entered as a cycle-maker from Coventry. His description tallied with that of Mr. Beale as far as being a little, stout, reddish-haired, middle-aged man, though both clerk and porter ridiculed the idea of mistaking the one for the other.

The manager turned very sharply, almost as though with a start, when the Chief Inspector stopped him a little later with:

"I believe, sir, that a Mr. Sikes of Coventry often comes to your hotel. Was he here yesterday?"

The manager, as so often to-day, hesitated before

answering the officer.

"I don't—I don't think so. No, no, I'm sure he was not. But why don't you look at the register?" This last in a tone of nervous irritation.

"Oh, he didn't stop in the house, but I thought he might have been in just the same."

"And what the devil has this Mr. Sikes to do with the affair which you are presumably investigating, Inspector?"

Pointer did not seem to hear the question, as with quick steps he passed on up the stairs and went at once in search of the housekeeper.

"Ah, I was on my way downstairs, but perhaps you can save me the trouble, Mrs. Green—" he beamed at her, and she beamed back at him, for he was a good-looking man.

"When Mr. Sikes was here on Saturday last, did you see him speaking to Mr. Eames at all?"

The housekeeper looked a little uncertain of her ground.

"Well, sir, I don't know the gentleman you're speaking of—Mr. Sikes—I haven't ever seen him."

"Not know Mr. Sikes?" Pointer's tone, though casual, showed his surprise.

"I've only been here two weeks, sir."

"Then you don't know the gentleman I mean even by sight?"

"I saw the manager and a gentleman whom he told me afterwards was a Mr. Sikes—but more than that I couldn't say, sir," and Mrs. Green, looking as though she would have preferred to say still less, tried to walk on, but he blocked the way.

"Just a moment. I particularly want to find out any friends of Mr. Eames, and I've reason to believe that he and this Mr. Sikes knew each other. The manager—I've just spoken to him"—Pointer was always glad to find even a crumb of truth which he could mix in with business—"doesn't remember whether Mr. Sikes went into Mr. Eames' room or not."

"You mean afterwards, sir?" Mrs. Green's suspicions of the police were again lulled. "The two gentlemen left Mr. Eames' room together and went on into the other balcony rooms. Mr. Sikes was looking for a room for his wife and family, but I had an idea —well, I thought the manager didn't want it talked about: you know he has to make special terms to some; but there, of course as he spoke to you about it, why, there can't be any harm in my referring to it—but whether the gentleman with him came back later and saw Mr. Eames or spoke to him downstairs is more than I can say; and now I must go, sir, or goodness knows what the girls will be up to in the linen-room." And go she did this time.

A message reached Watts on his return from rescuing the family hats from the monkeys which caused him to take the evening train to Coventry, there to learn as much as possible about its doubtless worthy citizen, Sikes.

Miller, who had been sent across to have a chat with the porters of the large block of flats opposite, brought back no grist for the official mill. But he had allowed it to leak out, in accordance with instructions, that there had been a robbery at the Enterprise, and that "the party interested" would pay for any information as to the thief who had escaped, possibly with a bag, either by way of the balcony or by the little side-door on Saturday afternoon.

"It's going to be a regular November Special," Pointer said to O'Connor on his return to his rooms, "or all the signs deceive me."

"D'ye mean to tell me that the criminal is still at large after all this time—close on twenty-four hours! Let me have the facts, Watson; sure Sherlock Holmes will give you a leg-up with pleasure," and "Sherlock Holmes" assumed a judicial attitude.

Pointer carefully went over the knotty points unearthed during the day. "There's Cox . . ." the Scotland

Yard man was evidently telling over his pieces, "who takes a room at the Marvel and uses it for a couple of hours . . . he's in the centre of the puzzle. Yes, he's that little gold ball you can just see." He glanced up at the Chinese puzzle above his head.

"Why d'ye place him there? Because you found that wax vesta in his room?" grunted O'Connor, who was for the moment a profound pessimist. His stamp had just slipped on a valuable piece of leather.

"No, partly because the two men who talked with him speak of him as possibly an American. Mr. Beale is an American, and Eames' clothes looked to me like Yankee cut, besides his umbrella. Thank God, to-morrow's Monday. I'm a Christian man, but there are times when I could do without Sundays—here at home. There is where the foreign police score. I shan't forget that. Avery case when I was sent to Naples–"

"I know," yawned Jim; "it rained all the time, and as for the famous view of the Bay—why, Plymouth Harbour beat it by ten goals to none."

"I don't wonder there are so many hasty marriages," Pointer spoke in sad soliloquy; "a man does feel a wish sometimes to come home to something alive, something intelligent."

"She wouldn't have much intelligence if she let you find her at home," pointed out his friend dispassionately, damping some leather with a hot sponge preparatory to making a fresh start, and for a while there was silence.

"When Cox tapped on the window of No. 14 who did he expect would open it for him?" the Irishman asked suddenly. "Eames? Or d'you think he knew that Eames was dead, and wanted to meet an accomplice there? If so, who? Beale?"

"I've only one idea about Mr. Beale so far, but it's a fixed one," Pointer replied slowly. "For some reason he's playing a game of his own. Judging by his eyes, it's bound to be a crafty scheme, and by his mouth, it won't boggle at trifles. However, the shape of his head guarantees that it'll be a clever one."

"You're a wonder, Alf. Since you've gone in for those phrenological and graphological lectures at the Kindergarden there's no hiding anything from you. Can you tell me by the shape of my head what Mr. Grey will say to me when he sees how that tooling has been done? You can't! Well, I can! You might as well continue your sermon by the way. I'm helpless, I must listen to it."

His friend was far too canny to proceed.

O'Connor began again: "Was the crime, for of course you think it was a crime, you hope it was one, you sin-hardened man-hunter, was it meant to be discovered by Beale, or . . . by someone else? Was Eames' body placed in that locked wardrobe so that the wrong person shouldn't find it, or so that the right person should?" O'Connor had given up all pretence at working and tried to read the answers to his conundrums one by one on Pointer's face, who finally answered a little wearily:

"Only time can tell, but as I said last night, frankly I'm puzzled as to what Mr. Beale with his position— for as I said I haven't a doubt but that he's all he claims to be—and his dollars are doing in this business of a shabbily-dressed young man who puts up in a single room at the Enterprise. Miller found out to-day that Mr. Beale didn't make any inquiries for rooms at the smarter hotels, but only applied in Southampton Row."

"Had he tried the Marvel?"

"No, he seems to've worked from the other end."

"Look here, you don't suspect him of being the actual murderer, do you?" O'Connor asked guilelessly.

Pointer pursed his lips. "Not the kind of man to do that sort of thing himself, I should judge, yet the way the job was done"—he trailed off into silence.

"Supposing it was he, and not Sikes, who was at the hotel earlier in the day, why should he come back in the evening? D'ye suppose he thought of those finger-prints of his which he had left everywhere, and wanted to have a chance to make them openly, as it were?" Judging by the detective's face he thought but poorly of this suggestion.

"You say the smaller footmarks, those on the canvas and on the doorstep about fitted Beale's slippers, didn't you?" persisted the other.

"As far as size goes—yes. Mr. Beale *could* have—though it would seem a mad risk to take—still he *could* have gone back upstairs again, when he left us last night in No. 14, and got out on to the balcony through the landing-window. But to get out with an umbrella and a raincoat would have been a feat he didn't look up to, though you never can tell. When I saw him a little later in the manager's room he certainly hadn't been clambering about in the rain."

"Well, his departure looks to me very fishy," maintained O'Connor in a tone which suggested that Pointer had steadily upheld it as a proof of the absent man's innocence. "What made him bolt out of the window?"

"I think he saw Cox pass by and recognised him."

"Suppose he and the manager are in it together? It was the manager who put Beale into No. 14. Perhaps Beale knew it was empty and the inquiries at the other hotels were only a blind."

The Irishman revelled in these talks early in a case, when there were not sufficient facts to hamper his idle fancy in its flights.

"Ah, as for the manager—" Pointer walked up and down the room. "That bit of acting about that green and white striped paper was badly enough done."

"So badly that it was creditable to him, eh?"

". . . And as for not discussing Eames' death with Mr. Beale—well, was it likely! When our expert tells me how much of that ash is Mr. Beale's cigars and how much the manager's cigarettes—he doesn't smoke cigars —I shall know better how much time those two spent hobnobbing together. At any rate something has changed the manager overnight. Then he acted like—well, if not an innocent man, then at least like a man who feels himself safe."

"Perhaps this bolt of Beale's has made the manager, too, think him guilty."

"He should tell us his reasons, then," the police-officer spoke very firmly. "Whatever it is, to-day he's all nerves, afraid to commit himself as to the day of the week."

"I wonder if he left some clue lying around in that room No. 14 and has recollected it during the night?"

"He needn't worry if it's that," Pointer spoke bitterly, "unless it's tagged: 'This is a Clue; don't miss ME!' I shouldn't see it. Too much fog about."

"Oh, come now," persisted his friend, "you've done jolly well so far—going at once to the Marvel and ferreting out about Cox. I don't know that I should have thought of that myself," he added handsomely.

"Well, true, I've not fallen far below you as yet," agreed Pointer in a cheered-up tone of voice. "I've already lost Mr. Beale, missed Cox, and can't find Eames' bag nor any trace of its whereabouts."

The two men laughed.

"As for Mr. Smalltoes,—I mean the man who stood on the canvas and walked out and then back through the little side door—I don't know where to place him yet. Centre or circumference."

"You mean Beale?"

"He may prove to be, but Mr. Beale picks his feet up as neatly as a water-rail; this man dragged his along. Mr. Beale wears pointed shoes; this man had on curious 'reformed' or 'true-shaped' boots. Straight on the inside and curving sharply about in a semicircle. Here's the outline." He held it out to O'Connor, who asked:

"What are the manager's feet like?"

"Two sizes larger. Well, this case is going to make or break me. I feel it in my bones."

Next morning Pointer was early at the Yard mapping out the day's campaign. As he expected, on telegraphing to the American Embassy he was assured that Mr.

Augustus P. Beale, a sub-editor and part proprietor of the *New York Universe,* a small gentleman, very bald, with reddish moustache, and gold fillings in his front teeth, was one of the States' choicest ornaments, a man of vast wealth and many interests. To clinch matters, one of Lester's snapshots was sent off to the Embassy, who sent back an immediate reply that this was undoubtedly the Mr. Beale whom all Americans abroad had been instructed to honour. If he were missing, he must be missed, until such time as it might please him to re-appear.

"Just so," sighed Pointer as he hung up the receiver. His first outing was to the small confectioner-tobacconist near the hotel which he had marked in his yesterday's rambles.

"Any letter for Mr. Eames? He's ill."

The man behind the counter stared at him suspiciously, but Pointer planked down a half-crown "and if you'll look after any letters for me, too—Charles Rowntree—for a while I'll be much obliged. Yes, Mr. Eames' cold has got a bit too bad for him to come out." Whistling blithely, he bent over a comic paper.

The man behind the counter softened. "What name did you say, sir? Mr. Charles Rowntree? Very good. Of course, strictly speaking, I might get into trouble if it got known; but there, why not be obliging? That's my motter. Mr. Eames' cold was pretty bad on Saturday, and what with the rain Saturday night—" He laid a letter down. Pointer handed over a penny, and bought a shilling packet of cigarettes before he left the shop. Eames' future correspondence would be sent on to the Yard, but any back numbers were equally valuable.

He opened the thin envelope, postmarked Dover, and drew out a sheet of paper ruled in squares.

"August 4th.
Wire me what's wrong. Be careful."

That was all, but the handwriting was the same as that on the Marvel's register. This document was carefully placed in the Chief Inspector's pocketbook.

At the Enterprise a man from the Yard was waiting for him with a wire from Watts. It appeared that Sikes the cycle-maker had left Coventry ten months ago. Should he try to trace him?

Pointer sent an affirmative reply, and listened to Miller's report. This time there had been no disturbance of any kind during the night, and the Chief Inspector could pass on quickly to the looking up of the two women who occupied rooms Nos. 11 and 12, the rooms nearest to No. 14. As to the other numbers, who were known to the hotel, Pointer left them to Miller.

Number eleven, nearest to the stairs, was occupied by a Mrs. Willett, a brightly painted lady whose diamonds and startling dresses turned every head, literally but not figuratively, as she tripped past on stilt-heels. Her age was a subject of some speculation. It was generally agreed, in spite of flashing teeth and gold brown hair, that forty would be nearer the mark than twenty.

She told Pointer quite frankly that she had been a smart dressmaker years ago, and now lived on the successful investing of her profits—partly in London, partly travelling.

"To Monte Carlo," he added mentally. She had been in the lounge nearly all of Saturday morning writing letters, and all of Saturday afternoon at the theatre. She had never seen anyone pass her window going towards No. 14.

"We want to find out if the gentleman—Mr. Eames— had any friends or acquaintance in the hotel. People often don't like to come forward in a suicide case," Pointer explained.

Mrs. Willett closed her black eyes convulsively.

"Don't," she begged. "I'm leaving the hotel as soon as I can make other arrangements. I had meant to leave Sunday morning, but some friends to whom I was going have a child down with the measles; but stay on here I can't—it's too terrible . . . such a shock . . . poor young man!"

Pointer agreed that it was terrible, and bowed himself out, thankful that the interview was over; for with her arch gestures, and frenzied vivacity, and her screaming, high-pitched voice, she exhausted the air of any room. He found the inmate of number twelve quite a change. Low-voiced, gentle-mannered Miss Leslie was a hard-working young actress, who had just got into a good part at one of London's leading theatres by sheer merit and hard work. She had been away all Saturday morning rehearsing, and all afternoon on the river with friends. She had never heard voices from Mr. Eames' room since he had taken it, nor had she ever seen anyone pass the window from Mr. Eames' room in either direction; but as she had not returned from her Saturday outing till seven o'clock, when she had taken off her sodden things and crept immediately into bed, she had not been in the hotel during the afternoon hours which interested the police most.

Much of this Pointer knew from his and Watt's examination of her room and wardrobe, while she had been at her bath yesterday morning, and from questions downstairs. Her wet clothes were noted in the little book the Chief Inspector consulted now and again.

"You never heard any voices from next door, you say?"

"Not except Saturday evening. I heard men talking in very low whispers late that night. I suppose you were one of them."

"Humph! Have you a maid who might have been in here Saturday afternoon while you were absent? We are trying to find out if Mr. Eames had any acquaintances who visited him that last day."

"I have no maid." Miss Leslie spoke somewhat brusquely, and turned again to her writing as a sign that the interview was over,—which was a mistake.

Pointer returned to No. 14—until the inquest, which had been fixed for Tuesday, the room was being kept by the police—and entered a few notes. Then he rang for the Boots, a thick-set young man with a humorous mouth and an intelligent eye. Pointer offered him a cigar and a match.

"Look here, Seward, between ourselves, who looks after the young lady in No. 12, Miss Leslie? She must have some sort of a maid surely."

The Boots lit his cigar appreciatively.

"Well, I don't want to get anyone into trouble, I don't, and of course I don't *know* anything about it"—he paused dramatically, but the police-officer said nothing —"and the housekeeper she really doesn't know anything about it; but I have heard the other girls say that Maggie earns a good many half-crowns from the lady for doing odd bits of mending and hooking her in her dresses, and then waiting up for her and hooking her out of them. But I don't want to get the girl into trouble, and the housekeeper has put her foot down more than once about the maids waiting on the ladies."

"You won't get her into any trouble"; and when the Boots had gone Pointer rang for Maggie the chambermaid.

"Look here, Maggie, you were the greatest help yesterday, and now I'm trying to find out more about Saturday afternoon itself. I can promise you that anything you say to me won't get to the housekeeper's ears; but were you ironing *all* Saturday afternoon? Come, now, I know that you *do* act as maid to Miss Leslie."

"Oh! she promised me not to tell—" began Maggie in a frightened voice.

"Weren't you part of the time in No. 12? It's your duty to speak up, you know, and I've told you that it shan't get you into any trouble."

She hesitated, then she began to cry.

"Oh, I know I ought to've told. I would have—I would have, reely, only for that dragon. You see, sir, I got the housekeeper to let me off part of the ironing on Saturday because of a headache, but after I'd laid down a bit it passed off, and I remembered a dress Miss Leslie particular wanted mended. So I didn't see why I shouldn't do it instead. What I mean to say, sewing isn't like ironing, is it, sir?"

Pointer said it sounded to him like a totally distinct form of occupation.

Maggie dried her eyes and began to recover her *aplomb*.

"What time did you go to Miss Leslie's room?"

He saw her eyes waver, and steadied her with, "It won't go any further, you know."

"Well, it was about ten past three, as near as might be, I suppose."

From her half-sheepish tone he guessed that the lying-down had been more mental than physical.

"And you were in the room till six?"

"Well-1, about that." She gave her head a little toss. "I can't think how you nosed it out." Then her tone melted: "But there, I've wanted to tell you about it, only I didn't dare. What I mean is, if the housekeeper knew of my arrangement with Miss Leslie—" She paused.

"Tell me what you heard or saw on Saturday." His tone invited confidences.

"Well, I only heard Mr. Eames moving about, and then I heard the clink of a glass on the marble washstand. I knew what that was—he was taking his tonic as I'd seen him do in the morning the day before. Very regular in his habits he was—the poor young gentleman."

Pointer leant forward in his chair. "Maggie, shut your eyes and think yourself back again in Miss Leslie's room. Don't forget anything, however trifling: it might be of the greatest help in getting at Mr. Eames' friends. Just shut your eyes and live Saturday afternoon over again out loud. You've just heard the clink of Mr. Eames' tumbler on the washstand—"

His rapt attention stimulated the girl. She, too, sat forward on her seat, shut her eyes, and locked her fingers.

"—then I heard him give a sort of exclamation, or more like a choke—I mean to say, it sounded like a bit of both"—she was evidently trying to live the hours over again—"and then I heard him drop into his arm-chair; it creaked as though he had fairly fallen into it. After that I heard nothing more for a long while. You know how hard it rained day before yesterday, and what a noise it made coming down, then I wasn't paying any attention—I mean to say I little thought—"

"You heard him drop into his chair"—Pointer's voice was almost hypnotic—and next—?"

"Nothing for a long while. Then I heard his door shut. Ah, thinks I to myself, he's gone downstairs as usual at four-thirty to the lounge for his tea—tea is included in the board here, you know, sir,—but it must have been him back after 'phoning to the office. Anyhow, I heard him lock his door, and then moving about, opening and shutting drawers very quickly and softly. Like this"—she jumped up and began to open and shut the tabledrawer, with quite a pause between—"packing, I'm sure, sir, which shows that he did mean to go into the country—"

"Never mind what it shows. Sit down and shut your eyes again. You heard him opening and shutting drawers—"

"Oh, yes, and I heard him moving about, too, but so light! I couldn't hear any footsteps, only all the floors here creak fearful. Then"—she went quite pale and fixed a genuinely horrified stare on the Chief Inspector—"I heard him pull the wardrobe out from the wall. I listened to that, of course, sir, for that *did* catch my ear—what I mean to say, the furniture being my lookout, so to speak, I noticed the way he tugged it. *That'll* mark the carpet, I thought to myself. Little did I—"

"After the pulling out of the wardrobe, what then?" Pointer's voice was intentionally matter-of-fact.

"Well"—she seemed puzzled as to how to put her recollection into words—"it sounded just as though he dragged the armchair about the room, but so—so—as if it

were so heavy, scraping and creaking, and then— then"—
her eyes dilated—"I heard the most awful sounds of the
chair straining and—and a sort of knocking sound, and
yet sort of dragging—oh, sir, I suppose he had just
stopped his packing and taken the poison then, and what
I heard was his death agonies—if only I'd known, I might
have run for a doctor!"

"No, no, Maggie, no one could have helped him. He
had taken too much poison."

"And to think I wondered what larks he was up to in
there! Then all got quieter, though I could still hear sort
of rustling sounds—what I mean to say, creepy sort of
noises, so quiet-like; and then I heard him shove the
wardrobe back against the wall, scraping it more than
ever, and that's what I don't understand. How could he do
that after taking the poison and all?"

"He may have felt better for a little while," suggested
the man from Scotland Yard.

"Well, I know I very nearly went in to speak about his
hauling the furniture about like that. I should have, only
I was supposed to be lying down. Then I heard the French
window opened. I suppose, as you say, sir, he felt a bit
better and stood there for a breath of air, but the rain was
coming down so just then that I couldn't be sure what I
heard. I had the blind down, it had some over so dark,
and was working by the electric light. I didn't hear
anything more, for which I'm thankful; I mean to say, I
don't think I could stand it to've heard him shut himself
into that wardrobe—it's quite bad enough to've heard
what I did. When I went in to get the room ready for Mr.
Beale the window-catch was open, though the window
had blown shut. To think that when I was getting the
room ready I actually tugged at the door of that
wardrobe. My goodness, if it *had* opened!"

"You heard nothing more?"

"Nothing, sir. Not a sound."

"You didn't hear Mr. Eames walk up and down on the
balcony or pass your window?"

"The rain was pouring so just then, sir, that he might have shouted and I shouldn't have heard anything outside. What I mean to say, it really was a clatter which came on just then, so as you couldn't hardly hear yourself think."

"You didn't look out at all after the blind was down?"

"Oh, no, sir, I had a rush to get the dress done in time as it was."

"Humph." Pointer seemed in no hurry to speak. The Eames case was to remain a "suicide" as long as possible.

"How were you sure it was Mr. Eames? I mean when you heard the glass clink? It might have been some friend of his in there at first?"

"I heard him sneeze when I had scarcely sat down. He had such a bad cold. I think myself that it was the influenza that made him go off his head and drink poison and all. I mean to say I've read of such cases."

"It looks very like it," he agreed, "and now, Maggie, I think I heard Miss Leslie go out a little while ago?"

"Yes, sir. She's due at a rehearsal at the Columbine."

"Then seat yourself in her room and listen. I shall drop something on the table, then I shall drop something else on it. I want you to come back and tell me which of the two sounds the heaviest. Listen carefully."

Maggie disappeared. Pointer could hear the wicker easy-chair creak slightly. He dropped one of the dental works which Eames had always had out on his table. Then after a pause he dropped it again. He and Watts had already tested just how much could be heard through the partition wall, but this time he was testing Maggie's accuracy.

She came back a second later, looking rather awkward.

"Well, sir, they both sounded alike. I mean to say I reely couldn't tell any difference, not to speak of."

"That proves they were both about the same weight, which is quite likely. Now, Maggie, go back again; sit where you sat on Saturday afternoon. I shall drop into this easy chair. I want to find out if the chair makes as much noise with me as it did with Mr. Eames. I mean to say"—the Superintendent bit his lip for a second —"that time you heard Mr. Eames fall into it, after he had taken his medicine. Knock once on the wall if it's not so loud, and twice if it's louder."

He listened till he heard Maggie draw up her chair, then he dropped heavily into his. Maggie knocked once. He let himself fall with all his weight, and Maggie came in.

"That's as near as no matter, sir, to the sound poor Mr. Eames made."

Pointer weighed fourteen stone and Eames he had guessed as under ten. The drug must have acted very quickly.

"And now I want to move about the room and see if I can make as little noise as Eames did later on—when you heard him come back and lock his door."

Maggie changed rooms again. Pointer took off both boots. He prided himself on his light footwork, and walking like Agag he crept around the room. Maggie knocked twice. He tried again. Again she knocked twice and then came in.

"Oh, you made ever so much more noise, sir, but then you'd make four of poor Mr. Eames. With him I didn't hear steps at all."

"You didn't hear my steps either surely," Pointer insisted, as he relaced his boots.

"Perhaps not as steps, sir, but, dear me, with Mr. Eames on Saturday I could only hear a drawer being pulled out ever so gently and then shut, after a minute almost without a sound, as you might say. If it hadn't been for the boards creaking and papers rustling, I couldn't have believed there was anyone in there, part of the time."

"Papers rustling. As though they were being scrunched up, or turned over like this?" He illustrated both sounds with a newspaper.

Maggie nodded as he refolded a sheet and drew it out of a make-believe envelope.

"That's the sound, sir, but there's the housekeeper's bell. And for goodness' sake don't let her know that it was I who said anything to you about that man who looked like the other gentleman. She told us someone had been chattering and that the management wouldn't have it. Of course, I said like the others that it wasn't me."

"You mean about Mr. Sikes, whom you thought was Mr. Beale?"

She nodded. "Shall I come back here when she's finished giving out the towels?"

But Pointer shook his head. "Hardly worth while. By the way, what time did Miss Leslie get back the day before yesterday? Pretty late, wasn't it?"

"I don't know when she got back, sir. I found her in bed when I came to do her room, which I always leaves till last so that the water will be fresher. She did have a time on the river in all that wet. Rotten it must have been. I don't wonder she didn't want to stick it out."

"What time did you go into her room on Saturday evening, did you say?"

"After I had finished doing this one up for Mr. Beale. About eight o'clock."

"Had you been in there after you left it at six?"

"No, sir." The maid's eyes showed her wonder at the course of the questioning.

"We're still hoping to find out Mr. Eames' friends, and it's possible that someone may have been in here on Saturday to see him. That's why I asked about Miss Leslie. She might have heard a knock." He handed the maid half-a-crown. "If you remember anything else let me know. However insignificant."

"I will, thank you, sir," and Maggie closed the door behind her.

After lunch the results of the autopsy reached the Chief Inspector. Morphia had been drunk in a quantity which made the police-officer open his eyes. It would be difficult for anyone but a chemist to lay his hand on such a solution. "There is one thing," the doctor's scribble finished, "that dose could never have had its taste disguised. Or at least it would have been uncommonly difficult."

All this was what Pointer had expected, but Maggie's account of what she had heard in No. 14 gave, for the first time, a clearer pattern to the kaleidoscope. Whoever had shut and locked Eames' door—about four-thirty—had entered from the corridor and not by the window which she had heard opened much later.

So, in general terms, from four to six was the time an alibi would have to cover.

CHAPTER FOUR

Miller had nothing suspicious to report in the actions of those inmates of the balcony rooms who had already visited the hotel on the other occasions. He was told off to test Mrs. Willett's alibi as far as that was possible from the hall-porter, while Pointer took a bus to a smart little bungalow in Sheen, where he hoped to find a lady, whose postcard, signed Mint, had been duly copied by the police and replaced in Miss Leslie's little bureau. It had run:

"Jack will call for you to-morrow in the car at two o'clock as you can't make it earlier, and we will be all ready for you in the launch. Hope the weather will be fine. Mint."

The "to-morrow" referred to had been the Saturday of Eames' death. A few inquiries told him that the bungalow belonged to a Major Thompson, whose record he promptly looked up in the local free library. The Major was now working at the War Office, after distinguished war services.

Mrs. Thompson was in, and very grave the Chief Inspector looked as he bowed to that young matron.

"Mr. Deane?" She glanced up inquiringly from the professional card sent in to her, which explained its owner as Mr. Deane, a solicitor of Grey's Inn Road.

"Excuse my call, Madame, but a client of ours had a motor accident on Saturday last,—August fourth. A car ran into his, and passed on without stopping near Richmond Park. You may have heard of it?" He looked at her with a legal air of being sure to find her out should she attempt any prevarication.

"I? No!"

"My client believes that he can identify the car that

ran into his by the fact that he recognised a Miss Leslie in it, who is playing at the Columbine Theatre. From inquiries made at the theatre it appears that the gentleman who was driving the car in question must have been Major Thompson."

"But our car didn't run into anything," protested the lady. "I drove it myself all morning. And, besides, my husband and Miss Leslie weren't anywhere near Richmond Park. What time is this accident supposed to've happened?"

Mr. Deane looked pained.

"My client, Madame, was run into at between half-past four and a quarter to five."

"There you are!" exclaimed Mrs. Thompson in triumph. "Major Thompson—he's out on the links this afternoon—fetched Miss Leslie about two o'clock from the Columbine, and drove her here, where my son and I were waiting in the launch. We had intended to go for a picnic up the river, but the weather was so shocking that we gave it up, and played bridge instead. Miss Leslie refused to let my husband or son take the car out again, and took a taxi back to her hotel just before dinner."

"So Miss Leslie was here in the house at the time my client's car was run into—about half-past four?"

Mrs. Thompson turned a deep red.

"Miss Leslie was here from two-thirty till she left about half-past seven," she said very distinctly. "If you care to go up to the golf links you'll find my husband there and the car! You can examine both at your leisure."

"Madame, I regret to say that I do not understand the affair at all." Mr. Deane stroked his grey moustache and spoke testily. "My client told me that he recognised Miss Leslie distinctly, and at her hotel, where of course I went first before venturing to disturb you, I was told that she had arrived on Saturday in a condition—I refer to her habiliments—which distinctly corroborated the idea of an accident."

Mrs. Thompson's foot was beating a light tattoo on the

floor, and there was a distinct sparkle in her pretty eyes as she looked at her visitor.

"I suppose she had a break-down in the taxi; I only know that she left here at half-past six, looking just as usual. She refused to borrow an umbrella. And now I must really refer you to my husband. You can't miss the links."

Mr. Deane excused himself stiffly for the intrusion, and let himself follow the road to the nearest telephone booth, at a pace that began with Mr. Deane's leisurely stride, and finished up in Pointer's best seven-leagued style. The number of the Sheens' golf club was in use. He requested to be rung up when it was free, and passed the time in entering notes in his little book. When he was put through he asked for Major Thompson.

"He's out on the links," replied a voice.

"Mrs. Thompson isn't quite sure if he got her message clearly." He heard an impatient tongue click.

"As I just explained to the lady, sir, the Major has absolutely forbidden any messages to be sent on to the links. I'm very sorry, sir."

Pointer was not.

"I see. Mrs. Thompson couldn't quite make out your explanation. I'll make it clear to her." And Mr. Deane, smiling cheerfully, took a bus to the club, which presented the usual picture of an August desert. He announced that he was waiting for the Major, and ordered tea on the balcony. Towards the close of his leisurely meal two figures clattered up the steps. A steward approached the shorter and indicated the visitor. The man came forward.

"I'm Major Thompson. You wish to see me? Shall I have tea at your table, or will it wait till afterwards? Tea I must have."

Mr. Deane strongly supported the idea of tea at his table. He produced his card and spoke of his client's accident.

"I've just come from Mrs. Thompson; she requested

me to see you." There was no doubt as to Major Thompson's embarrassed bewilderment.

"Oh—ah—I see. But didn't my wife explain—" he gazed wildly around for his tea.

"No, Major Thompson, she did not. The onus of proof rests on you." And Mr. Deane fixed his pince-nez more firmly on his nose, and eyed the man across the table.

"Well, but—by jove—my wife told me—I mean Miss Leslie"—the major saw salvation and snatched at it— "you should see Miss Leslie. Miss Leslie is the person—"

"Not at all." Mr. Deane stiffened. "My client was only able to identify the young lady, it is true, but she only comes into the case as identifying or not your car."

"I see. Well, then, it's all quite simple. I never was anywhere near Richmond Park at the hour you mention."

"Nor your car?"

"Go and have a look at the old bus. There isn't any paint on her to scratch, but the mud of centuries ought to do as well. If you can find any dent on her—ah, here's my tea. I see you had shrimp sandwiches, too. Shows this isn't your first visit here, eh?"

But Mr. Deane was not to be diverted.

"My client," he began with his dry, preparatory little cough, "fixes the hour at about four-thirty, or a little later. If you will kindly state—with, of course, some— ah—proofs—that neither you, Miss Leslie, nor the car were near Richmond Park at the hour of the collision, the matter would drop, as far as you are concerned. It must be, of course, a simple matter for you to establish your whereabouts at the time in question."

The major drank long and deep. Then he placed his empty cup in its saucer with something of a bang.

"I was playing bridge with my wife and friends at home, Miss Leslie had gone on to some friends, and the bus was in my garage. I fetched Miss Leslie, who is an old school-friend of my wife's, at two o'clock from the Columbine, as you say they told you at the theatre, and drove her home to Richmond. We had intended to go on the river, but my wife refused to go out in the launch on account of the look of the sky, and suggested bridge instead. Miss Leslie didn't seem to care for cards and decided to taxi on to some friends. So we put her into a cab—she refused to let us take her in the car—and off she went about a quarter to three. And as I haven't seen her since, she couldn't have been with me at four-thirty near any park."

Mr. Deane tapped his teeth reflectively.

"Um—m. I'm afraid—my client claims pretty heavy damages—his car's a wreck, though he says that the one which ran into him was barely dented. And about Miss Leslie—I understood that Miss Leslie said she was with you and your wife all afternoon. I think there's some mistake—I think there is."

The major began to show signs of distress. He dropped a sandwich, but Mr. Deane foiled that time-honoured device to gain time by instantly bringing his foot down on it with a vigour surprising in one of his deliberate movements. The major cast one sulky glance on the savoury morsel adhering to his visitor's boot, and gulped down a word or two. He took up the last sand- wich, but after a glance at Mr. Deane's general attitude of "ready," sat munching it with a thoroughness which would have moved the late Mr. Fletcher himself to admiration.

"Well, sir?" asked Mr. Deane tartly.

The major chewed on in silence. Finally there was no help for it; he had to swallow the last crumb, but no shipwrecked sailor could have done so more lingeringly.

"Well, of course, if Miss Leslie said so—of course she was. I suppose I've got it muddled. As a matter of fact— now I think of it—of course we all played bridge all afternoon."

"*All* afternoon?" repeated Mr. Deane, as though unable to believe his ears.

"No, no, no!" corrected the hapless major, "just till about—about—oh, hang it all, I never notice time when I am at cards. But as a matter of fact, I believe we left off quite early—that is, relatively, you know. Every's relative nowadays, thanks to old Einstein—what?"

Mr. Deane sat awhile in silence. The two were quite alone on the balcony. He decided that the time had come for him to make way for the Chief Inspector. It was a pity, for Mr. Deane had thoroughly enjoyed himself. When he spoke, his voice had changed totally.

"I have something I would like to say to you, sir. Would you mind walking out on to the links with me?"

The major gave him a penetrating glance.

"Certainly. Come this way." They strolled off into utter silence and safety from eavesdropping.

"C.I.D. man, eh?" asked the soldier. "Anything wrong at the Office?"

"No, sir, not to my knowledge. I am Chief Inspector Pointer, of the Yard, as you guessed. I'm on a queer suicide case which has taken place at the hotel Miss Leslie is stopping at—the Enterprise—in the room adjoining hers, in fact. We hope to keep it out of the papers till the inquest on Wednesday. Now, as you, of course, know, sir, every case of suicide that isn't as clear as daylight has to be sifted by us pretty thoroughly. Part of the sifting in this case is to place the people's where-abouts who were on the same floor—the first floor. It's a question, roughly, of the hours between four to six on last Saturday afternoon. Miss Leslie is among the other people. You quite understand, sir, that it's a mere matter of form, that we know from the hotel employees that she wasn't in the hotel till much later in the day; but that isn't enough. We must try to have alibis for everyone on the floor between those hours, if it's a possible thing; and if it isn't, we must know why it isn't. Now, sir, can you tell me where Miss Leslie *really* was during those hours?"

Major Thompson thought awhile.

"I don't know that I care to make any statement in so serious a matter as this," he said finally. "Miss Leslie will give you any information you ask for—any that you have a right to—I am quite sure," and he turned away.

Pointer stopped him.

"Ah, but I can't explain things to Miss Leslie. Not a soul must know that the case isn't a perfectly clear suicide. That's why I adopted my little ruse with you just now, sir. I should have preferred not to have told even you about the matter. Doubtless the young lady would explain her movements on Saturday afternoon, if she knew why I am interested in them; but as I can't explain my reasons to her, I doubt very much if she won't refuse to tell me anything."

"I see." The major again thought awhile. "Yes, I see your point, Inspector, though I owe you something for pulling my leg in that unconscionable way, and stepping on the choicest sandwich."

Pointer repressed a grin.

"I'll be quite frank with you. There was Miss Leslie, my wife, my son Henry, and my son's fiancée at the bungalow on Saturday afternoon. My wife and the other young lady decided—very sensibly—that the weather was much too threatening for an outing on the river, but Miss Leslie, for some whim, tried to insist on our taking the launch out. Henry, of course, backed her up, like an idiot. My wife refused to go, the young lady refused to go—I kept myself out of it all by cleaning the car"—the major glanced at the disreputable old Armstrong, stiff with mud, which was standing a few yards from the two men—"and the upshot was that Miss Leslie and Henry decided to go in the launch, while my wife and Edith went into the house to get tea ready for them when they would return. I saw the silly young optimists off, and we expected them back within a quarter of an hour. But not a bit of it! Henry was beginning to see what a fool he was, but a girl doesn't see reason so quickly. It was nearly seven o'clock before the two returned, soaked through, of course. Miss Leslie has some friends higher up the river: they had pulled up there, had tea with them, and then made for home in all that downpour! After that, she took a taxi from our house and went back to her hotel; and if you know of a madder way of spending last Saturday afternoon, I don't. My wife is furious with her, and Edith is furious with my son."

"I'm afraid I must ask for the name of the friends with whom Miss Leslie had tea," murmured Pointer.

The major reluctantly gave it him, and the two men parted on good terms.

What in the world had induced a rising young actress to spend her time in such an extraordinary manner, mused the police officer as he took the bus on to-the Blacks, where Miss Leslie had tea.

The villa was shut up, and, what was more, had been shut up since the middle of July, so the nearest tradesman told him. The Blacks were away at Cromer.

Again Pointer 'phoned to Major Thompson. This time to his home address. The Blacks were "out," he explained. Might he call and see Mr. Henry Thompson?

"What's wrong now?"

"Nothing, sir. Merely that I want to get hold of someone who was actually with Miss Leslie between four and six o'clock," soothed the Chief Inspector.

The major grunted.

"He's not here now, but I believe you'll find him at the Sesame Club this evening about eight o'clock," and the receiver snapped up. Evidently the domestic affairs of Henry were not yet running smoothly.

In the Sesame lounge at seven-thirty Mr. Deane presented himself. Mr. Thompson was in the writing-room, he was told.

Mr. Deane produced his card, and with it the tale of the motor collision.

"I've met your father on the links this afternoon. Major Thompson very kindly gave me your address here—he's certain that you can give Miss Leslie an alibi for the hour in question at any rate. That would clear matters up a great deal."

"Of course she wasn't in our car. She wasn't in any car," grunted young Thompson; "no such luck. We were—

having tea with friends," he finished lamely. Mr. Deane raised an eyebrow.

"The Blacks' house has been shut up for three weeks."

The young man swung around on his chair.

"It's a perfectly rotten affair," he burst out at length; "my stepmother thinks I ought to've let Miss Leslie go out on the river by herself. But, you see, I knew,—I mean, I've known her all my life—besides, the weather didn't look half bad when we started"; and then followed a tale of a wilful young female dragging the reluctant male into boat and tea-shop, where they partook of a chilly tea— their friends' house proving shut up—and back home through the pouring rain. The afternoon had apparently not gained any retrospective charm in the young man's memory, but Pointer got the clue he was after. Miss Leslie—according to young Thompson —hoped to meet Malcolm Black, to whom she had been engaged before she had taken to the stage. Though the family were away, she had seemed quite confident that the house would be open, and that they would find Malcolm on the little island summer-house which belonged to them.

When Mr. Deane had dexterously turned the young man inside out, he left him, soothed by the sympathy of one man of the world for another, and quite unaware of the operation to which he had been subjected. As for himself, he had a possibly true explanation of those drenched garments, over which he and Watts had paused more than a moment during their investigation of all the wardrobes of the hotel.

The next day was the inquest—a purely formal affair, for the Coroner agreed with the police as to the wisdom of leaving out all possible details. He confined it, there-fore, to the reading aloud of the letter left by the deceased dentist, R. Eames, and to the doctor's testimony as to the huge amount of morphia taken. The hotel employees were only called on to identify the body, and then proceedings were adjourned for a fortnight, ostensibly to allow of the family of the young man being found and communicated with. The Chief Inspector also managed, on the same ground, that of further identification, to get the burial postponed until Saturday.

It was a busy day for the police. The work started yesterday of looking up the names of all arrivals from the Colonies or the United States in order to trace a Cox or an Eames, or any names fitting those initials, had to be continued, and the seven 'phone calls which had come through to the Enterprise about five o'clock were each minutely investigated. Three came from within a stone's throw of the hotel; but as the machine in question was in a large general shop, all efforts to identify the occupiers of the booth at about the hour given were in vain. Yet one curious fact came to light.

The lift-boy of Knotts, the shop in question, was certain that he had seen the Enterprise manager leave the 'phone box at about that hour.

The manager, questioned casually on the point, maintained that it was the day before—on the second— when he had 'phoned to his hatter, but the boy persisted that it was on Saturday and not on Friday, as he himself had his afternoon off on Friday.

The manager's hatter, when Pointer rang him up, could remember no call at all from the manager during the latter half of the week.

Pointer put it to him that there must be some mistake; "and, frankly, we want to weed out the telephone calls as far as possible."

"Sorry, but I suppose some shop assistant forgot to make a note of my message—or, stay, I do believe I didn't succeed in getting through."

Inquiry proved that there had been another call occupying the hatter's wire at five, and a little before, but the Chief Inspector wondered whether this were merely a lucky chance or not.

A telegram came from Watts during the morning: "Found Sikes. Denies visit to London. No alibi. Arriving four o'clock."

And punctually to the hour Watts presented himself at Pointer's room in the Yard.

"Sikes—revised version of Isaacs, I fancy, sir—lives in a handsome villa at Brighton—garage and fairly good car. Maidservants. I told him, as agreed, that a wealthy American had disappeared rather suddenly, and the Embassy was making cautious inquiries; that he had last been seen at the Enterprise Hotel, and that there was some doubt as to the time of his arrival. I gave a very flattering description of his looks"—Watts laughed—"and then said that the manager had given us to understand that it was himself—Mr. Sikes—and not Mr. Beale who had been seen at noon on Saturday in the hotel in company with the manager; and as he very much resembled Mr. Beale's description, we had come to him to clear the matter up once for all. I put it most tactfully, I assure you, sir; but he got purple and banged the table. 'Impudent lies! I never was near the place since March last. I don't care what the management says; I never was near the place on Saturday. Haven't been to London, except to a theatre, in months. Tell the Enterprise people that if they make any future mistake of the kind I'll have them up. I'll sue the manager, that's what I'll do!' He had heard about the whole business already from someone else, I'll swear, and was fed up with it."

"Humph! Well?"

"I got nothing more out of him, sir. I think his rage choked him too much to let him speak. As to an alibi —he said that his word was a sufficient alibi. He had gone early to town last Saturday, by the eleven o'clock, in order to buy his wife a present, had gone the rounds of the silversmith's windows, had seen nothing he liked; hadn't gone in to any shops, and had wound up the day with a theatre, after luncheon at Frascati's at one o'clock, and returned to Brighton by the five o'clock. Asked if he had seen anyone he knew, he went off the rails again, and shouted that he had made his money in business, and not in gadding about town making acquaintances with idlers. So that's that, sir."

"You verified his trains, of course?"

"Oh, yes, sir. They were all O.K. He was well known at the station."

"So that's that," echoed Pointer as Watts filed his report.

"Nothing connected with the manager seems to be quite straightforward. However— . . ." He told Watts of the shape the case had assumed since his absence.

"Maggie thinks she heard the *room* door—the corridor door—open. Whew!"

"It's lucky there was someone in number twelve Saturday afternoon. But for that, there would be no question of time. That medicine-bottle could have been tampered with as soon as Eames had taken his morning dose. Whoever did it poured out the medicine, poured in the morphia solution, which they doubtless flavoured with a little peppermint and eucalyptus like the medicine, and left it for Eames to help himself to, at a time when they might have been chatting with the Archbishop by way of an alibi. Then, when Eames was unconscious, someone enters, locks the door, takes out the back panels of the wardrobe, and fixes on the little brass bolt; shoves Eames in, dead or unconscious, screwed the panels into place again, emptied the bottle on to the balcony—it was pouring at the time—put back the last dose of medicine which they had taken out earlier in the day, goes through the dead man's papers and effects, and gets away with whatever the murder was committed for in the bag, down the service-stairs, and out into the street that way."

"Clever scheme!" Watts breathed, who was following his Superior's account with breathless interest.

"A simple one, for if it hadn't succeeded—if Eames hadn't drunk the medicine, but had disliked the taste and thrown it away—the poisoner could try again. As for Mr. Beale, we have had word from the American Embassy not to bring him in in any way."

"Do you think there's any chance of the affair turning out to be political, sir?" asked Watts. "The manager, you know, is Irish—Hughes—and Eames is an Irish name, and so is Beale."

"Let's hope for all our sakes it won't be that! If there's one thing that's calculated to break a policeman's heart first, and his career afterwards, it's a political case." The mere suggestion covered the Chief Inspector's face with gloom. "Tails all over the place you mustn't step on," he added, after a long pull at his pipe.

"Seen the picture of Eames in the late editions, sir?" asked Watts, laying one before him. "I don't call it a good likeness myself."

"As unlike him as they could make it," agreed Pointer.

"We've asked the Colonial papers to copy the picture, but much good a smudge like that will do."

"Something unforeseen may turn up from it, though," suggested Watts.

"Not in this case," corrected Pointer with conviction. "Everything unforeseen will have to be looked for with a searchlight, in my opinion;" and Watts was too much impressed by the medicine-bottle clue which Pointer had picked out to answer.

"Now, then, Watts"—the Chief Inspector turned to business again—"I want you to find out whether Beale, or the manager, or anyone corresponding to the description of Cox, has been buying any morphium in London. Take Eames' snapshot, too, though that's hardly likely to be needed." He went into careful details of the men and taxis he could have to help him.

For two days Watts searched London, but found nothing to prove that any of the three men had ever been near a chemist save Cox, that one time when he had bought the fatal bottle. Meantime nothing transpired at the Yard about Eames. Letters flowed in by the score purporting to recognise the printed likeness, but all the patient investigations of the police only proved that the recognition was mistaken. In Canada a terrific forest fire was raging, and under the circumstances the Yard could hardly press for larger space to be given to the picture of an unknown Englishman. At the Enterprise there had been practically no changes —at least from the first floor, and nothing had as yet transpired which could give the casting hither and thither police any definite trail.

"How's the manager developing?" O'Connor asked the night of Watts' return. "Been getting any deeper into your black books?"

"I've had a man look up his record—"

"Ah, well, that would be about the same thing with a policeman. Heaven help us all!"

"The report came in this afternoon. About a year ago he bought rather heavily of securities which are to-day a mere fraction of what he gave for them. He's slightly in the hands of money-lenders, and is altogether by no means as happily placed as might have been expected; for though the hotel is full, the running expenses are higher under him than were allowed for, and as his salary is only paid on net profits he must be pretty badly put to it sometimes. However, we've not been able to trace any previous acquaintance between him and Mr. Beale—not as yet.

"That scrap of green and white paper"—Pointer seemed to see it before him: "the manager isn't particularly quick-witted, but he certainly was quick-footed, for he was standing on it before you could say Jack Robinson—on the one and only piece of evidence the room contained. By the way, a jeweller to whom I showed Eames' studs says they're unusually fine pearls—for their size. Question is shall we ever learn what other things of value he may have had with him?"

There was a pause. "Our analyst reports that there were the ashes of two cigars and twelve cigarettes in the little lot I took him. That amount couldn't have been smoked in five minutes."

O'Connor had risen and laid an old copy of the *Era*

before him. "I thought I vaguely remembered something of the kind, so I hunted these up. What d'ye think of them?" he asked in would-be careless tones.

Pointer examined them. They were pictures of Miss Leslie taken four years back, in the character of an old man.

CHAPTER FIVE

It was late on the afternoon of Thursday that the Chief Inspector again went meticulously over every article of Eames' which he had in his safe. The watch he lingered over longest. His advertisement had brought in no helpful replies. He had taken the watch to a neighbouring goldsmith, who had only been able to tell him that the maker, a very poor one, had long ago given up work and life itself. Pointer laid it on one side for a moment and took up the waistcoat. It was a well-worn garment, with very small pockets, one of which —the watch-pocket—had a permanent bulge. He fitted the watch into it. As he looked at it attentively it struck him that the watch did not conform at all to the outline supposed to have been made by it. An idea came to the police officer. He put on a pair of magnifying glasses and scrutinised the inside of the back of the case long and minutely. Finally he rose, with a faint flush in his cheek, and took a taxi to the largest watchmakers and goldsmiths in London.

"Sorry," the manager said patronisingly when Pointer, after asking for a private room, had shown him the watch; "it's not the kind of article we ever deal in. Not our class at all." He handed back the watch contemptuously, and endeavoured to look over the other's head.

Pointer, unruffled as ever, opened the case again.

"Then you don't know that mark? Those crossed semicircles?"

He pointed to two almost invisible pin scratches.

The manager started, and took the watch again quickly.

"Two semicircles crossed? By Jove, so there are! The marks are so old and worn that I didn't notice them.

You've good eyes, Inspector."

"I look at what is before me," was the quiet reply, which the salesman greeted as a sally of wit.

"Ha, ha! We all do that, I suppose. Well, to tell you the truth, that happens to be an old private mark of our own."

"Just so. You changed it some twenty years ago."

"Oh—ah! You certainly are well up in your work! If you sit down again for a moment I'll make inquiries."

Some time went by before the manager returned.

"I can't trace the watch in the least. I think that mark must be a mistake, or a joke, though it's our own mark right enough." He was obviously puzzled.

"Could it be a watch you lent a customer in place of one left to be mended? Or what about your branch establishment in Bond Street?"

The manager left him alone again and returned to say that he thought the Chief Inspector's suggestion highly probable, but that they had no record, even so, of the watch on their books. He recommended him to try their branch.

Pointer thanked him and took another taxi.

At Bond Street he found that the manager had 'phoned, and he was shown at once into a little room where he found a salesman waiting for him.

"Chief Inspector Pointer? We've been going over our books. I think I may be able to help you."

The police-officer handed him his treasure. The man opened the case.

"Yes, this is a watch I let a young gentleman have" — he laid it down and ran his finger along a ledger— "last Saturday morning. As a rule, we furnish no watches to our customers, but in this case we supplied him with one as a makeshift for his own very valuable repeater."

"Was this the young gentleman?" Pointer held out Eames' photo. The salesman identified him after a long scrutiny. "He wore a brown tweed suit and a soft brown felt hat."

"That's him," muttered Pointer, drawing a deep breath.

"He gave the name of Eames. But his repeater, I have it here, has another family's coat of arms engraved on the back. Do you know anything about heraldry, Inspector?"

"A little."

"Well, of course, we have to, and besides—well frankly, the repeater was of a very superior kind, and the young man's clothes were not quite in keeping, you know what I mean?"

Pointer secretly damned any interest in clothes just then.

"Oh, quite! And the crest was?"

"I recognised it at once, but as a mere matter of form I looked it up, as I thought it is that of the Perthshire branch of the Erskine family. Here is the repeater." He laid it down beside the Scotland Yard man.

"And now, I presume, I may take back this. And what about the charge for the spring we supplied?"

Pointer assured him that that would doubtless be settled by the family. He asked the salesman how it was that he had missed the offer of a reward for the watch, and whether he had not noticed any likeness between his customer and the picture of the "Hotel suicide," let alone the name of Eames which had been given in the Press. The shopman smiled a little wearily.

"Stocktaking," was his laconic excuse, "and besides our three lending watches don't go by number any more. They're too ancient for that."

Pointer left the shop with a buoyant tread just as the shutters went up.

The Yard has its own short cuts, and after a couple of hours of strenuous trunk-calls, he was able to get into touch with a certain solicitor, a Mr. Russell, of Russell and Son, of Perth, who, when driven into a corner, finally admitted that he acted, since his father's retirement, as legal adviser to the particular branch of Erskines in whom the Yard was interested.

"It's about young Erskine who's come over from Canada lately—"

This seemed to galvanise the man at the other end. So much so that it was some time before Pointer could get his query through the Scotsman's ejaculations.

"He's dead. Suicide apparently. Could you identify the body?" With many repetitions he got a general description of "Eames" over the line. The watch clinched it. The invisible Russell said he would come to town by the earliest possible train. Then followed a little difference of opinion as to the exact meaning of that term, Russell pointing out that he said the earliest *possible*, while Pointer maintained time-tables to be the only standard. He won finally, and Mr. Russell agreed to take the midnight express south, leaving his office in the hands of his father.

He arrived at the Yard late the following afternoon, and almost in silence the two men drove to the chamber where "Eames" still lay in his patent ice-coffin.

Russell recognised him at once, and the Scotsman's air of almost suspicious reserve—as that of a man whose valuable time might be wasted—left him. Seated in the Chief Inspector's room at the Yard over a glass of his own mixing, Mr. Russell told all that he knew of the young man.

"You're quite sure, Mr. Russell, that you recognise the corpse?"

Pointer was writing swiftly. So was Watts.

"Aye, only too sure. I knew him as a boy well enough, and besides he's the very image of his father." He stared ruminatingly out of the window. "It's not easy to know how much I ought to tell you, Inspector Pointer. Under ordinary circumstances I should, of course, say nothing till I had talked with Mrs. Erskine— poor leddy! poor, poor leddy!—but as you say time is important—well, I've thought it over well coming down here, and I've decided to tell you the whole family story as far as it concerns young Robert Erskine. Their branch has been settled in

Perthshire since the battle of Flodden Field. His father—
Mr. Henry Erskine— was the owner of a fine bit of land
and fortune. He sold all the land long ago, all but a park
with the dower-house in it which was included in his
wife's settlements. She had a property of her own, too,
and comes of an equally good house. She was an
Abercrombie and is still alive. The father is dead. The
marriage, I fancy, was not an over great success. She is a
quiet, deeply religious body, and Mr. Erskine—well, he
liked concerts, and operas, and paintings, and travelling.
He had one younger brother Ian who had bought a large
ranch in Canada, and seventeen years ago—Robert was
then twelve—Mr. Erskine and his son went on a year's
visit to this brother. While there—I think it was only
after a couple of months,—Mr. Henry Erskine was
thrown from his horse and killed. By his will—I have a
copy of it here with me—he left the use of his property to
his wife during her life-time with remainder to his son
should he outlive her. In case of Robert Erskine's death,
before his mother, half was to become his wife's
possession absolutely, and the other half goes to found art
scholarships in Perth. In case both son and wife were
dead, the estate, it was worth about seven thousand a
year at the time of Mr. Erskine's death, and has since
greatly appreciated—to be split up into various art
scholarships at Scotch towns. His brother, Ian Erskine
was a wealthy man, a bachelor, who had expressed his
intention—in writing—of leaving his entire fortune to his
only nephew Robert. Do I make myself quite clear?"

"Oh, quite," breathed the two police officers, who were
lapping up the information thirstily.

"This uncle was appointed the boy's guardian, and
Robert was to remain with him until he should be of age.
By that time Mr. Ian Erskine had died, too, leaving his
fortune as he had promised, I understand, and Robert
stayed on at the Four Winds Ranch near Calgary. We had
very little indeed to do with him after his father's death. I
presume he preferred to employ his uncle's man of

business. I doubt but that he takes after his father and is a bit careless with money, for over two months ago, on May 20th to be exact, Mrs. Erskine instructed me to send Robert £1,000. I was abroad for my holidays at the time, so I went to see her. Mrs. Erskine lives in France for the sake of her health. She left Scotland shortly after her husband and son went to Canada and has a fine villa outside Nice. There she showed me his last letter, in which he asked for the money to settle some card debt. I gathered from Mrs. Erskine, more by what she didn't say than by what she did, that he frequently applied to her for funds. I'm not saying that she can't afford it, for owing to her profitable investments—she has a rare head for finance —her income has been more like ten thousand than seven these many years past. But, frankly, gentleman, it wasn't the kind of letter I should have cared to write to my mother,—and her a widow and frail. Well, we sent the one thousand pounds by a draft on a Toronto bank, and received a scrap of a receipt on June seventeenth, along with a sealed envelope marked 'My Last Will and Testament' with instructions to keep it for him, and use it if need be."

"Can I see the covering letter to his will?"

The solicitor held it out. It was the briefest of notes headed from a Toronto hotel and dated June 4.

"Dear Mr. Russell,
I shall be much obliged if you will take charge of the enclosed. It is my last, and only will. Should I die kindly act on it at once.
Faithfully yours,
Robert Ersktne."

"You have the will with you, too, sir?"

"Aye, I have." But Mr. Russell made no motion to produce it.

"Under the circumstances, as you have definitely identified the body as that of Robert Erskine, you would save us all a great deal of trouble, and yourself a long detention in London, by letting us have it now."

The lawyer pondered this for a moment. Then he drew out and broke the seals of a grey envelope. In it was a half-sheet of notepaper. By it Robert Erskine on June Fourth had left everything of which he might die possessed to one Henry Carter, of 10401 Street, Calgary.

"Alias Cox," was Pointer's silent comment as he passed it on to Watts. Then he compared it carefully with a letter which he took out of his safe, the note found on Eames' body. The writing tallied. He handed the note to the lawyer, who read it with emotion. For he and the young fellow in whose name it stood, were about of an age, and had known each other as children.

"To think of it! To think of the Perthshire Erskines ending like this! All their money and all their land to come to no better finish!"

Pointer pressed a button and had the will handed over to the Yard's experts to be photographed and enlarged.

"Now about this Henry Carter, who is he?"

"I never heard of him before in my life. He won't be a Perthshire man."

The Chief Inspector played with his fountain pen for a while.

"Do you think Mrs. Erskine could come over for the adjourned inquest? It won't be till a week from Tuesday?"

"I doubt it. Might kill her. She is a very delicate woman. Robert was her only child, you remember. Nor can I see the point. In his letter he says clearly enough that his intention is to commit suicide. And as for identification—she hasn't seen him since I have. He's never been back to Europe before. I know that."

"Did you know that he was coming?"

"My dear sir, I know as little of Robert Erskine's movements these last years as I do of the Pope. Barring that receipt for the thousand pounds, and that envelope with his scrap of a will inside, we haven't heard from him since his father died these many years ago. And at that

time it was my father who transacted the winding up of
the estate. I was but a lad."

"Well, I hope Mrs. Erskine will come. I must run over
to France, if not. She may be able to throw some light on
the reasons for her son's—ah—end. Now, Mr. Russell, do
you happen to know whether Mr. Robert or Mr. Ian
Erskine took any interest in politics out in Canada?"

"I do remember a letter my father read me, in which
Mr. Erskine—Mr. Henry Erskine—spoke of difficulties
his brother was having with some Communist settlers
near by; but what would that have to do with young
Erskine's suicide?"

"Nothing probably, but we must leave no stone
unturned. Well, Mrs. Erskine may know more. I should
like to find out what Robert Erskine's attitude on labour
questions was."

"But his letter—! Man, a young fellow is hardly likely
to kill himself for such like whimsies."

"True again, Mr. Russell; but as there doesn't seem
any reason lying around on the surface why a wealthy
young man should kill himself, we must poke about for
one. By the way, do you know how much his uncle left
him?"

"Mrs. Erskine wrote to the effect that he was now
wealthier than she. That's all I know."

"Thanks." The Chief Inspector drew Watts into
another room.

"Cable to the Toronto police for full particulars of
young Erskine and Cox. And repeat to Calgary police."
Pointer turned to his desk with the air of a man who has
still a full day's work before him, whatever the hands of
the clock might say about it.

Mr. Russell cleared his throat, but his courage
apparently failed him, as with a bow and a "See you
tomorrow at your hotel, Mr. Russell—at eleven, if that
hour suits you," the Chief Inspector was gone.

Mr. Russell cleared his throat again.

"Mr. Watts—I wonder, now—I'm wishful to see the

room where poor Robert Erskine took his life. I knew him as a boy, you see." There was genuine feeling in the Scotsman's face.

The detective opened the door. "Chief Inspector!" he called, but his superior was out of earshot.

Watts rubbed his chin.

"Well, sir, of course, strictly speaking, I should say no. But as you're in the case as it were, and a friend of the family—well, as it happens, I shall be at the Enterprise Hotel within the hour on business. I'll pick you up in the lounge there if you like, and let you just have a look at No. 14. The hotel doesn't intend to let it till Monday."

He was as good as his word, and took the solicitor up with him to the threshold of the fatal room. Mr. Russell shook his head slowly. "Pitiful, aye, pitiful indeed, to think of Robert Erskine come to such a pass that he was glad to take poison and shut himself up in yon box. Do you think there was a wumman at the bottom of it?"

"There often is," agreed Watts. Not until the adjourned inquest did the Yard intend a word to leak out which might suggest that the "suicide" was a murder.

"Aye, just so," murmured Mr. Russell as he tiptoed from the room.

On the stairs they met Pointer, who gave them both a baleful glare. Watts would have explained, but his superior silenced him with a gesture.

"Not out here. Mr. Russell, don't let us detain you, sir"; and the lawyer left the detective to a grim little interview back in No. 14.

"My aim was to keep the man's identity a secret, as I told you." The Chief Inspector's voice lost none of its edge for being carefully lowered; "and you bring the family solicitor to the hotel! Suppose the criminal is still in the house—you give him notice that we know who Eames was. Beale, or Cox, may both of them be staying under this very roof as Jones or Smith for aught we know!"

Watts bent to the blast, and apologetically took himself off, inwardly swearing that never again would he yield to a kindly impulse.

Pointer walked swiftly downstairs and knocked at the manager's door. He was greeted with rather forced cordiality.

"Mr. Manager, I asked you once before if Mr. Eames left anything in the safe. You said no. We have learned today that he may have had some hundreds of pounds with him. Are you sure of the honesty of your booking clerks?"

"Oh, quite! Absolutely." There was no mistaking the conviction in the manager's tones, but also no mistaking the fact that he had turned very pale.

"You have the only key to the safe, I understand?"

"That is so."

"I see." Pointer was watching him intently and not disguising the fact. "The night-clerk, Biggs, says that he happened to see you open the safe several times during the days Eames was here, and noticed a small sealed box, wrapped in green and white striped paper, on the top shelf to the right. He is certain that he saw it last on the night of the third—Saturday—when you opened the safe to give a Dutch gentleman back his deposit. On Sunday morning the safe was opened at nine o'clock to let a lady put in her jewels, and the box was gone. Can you tell me anything about that box?"

"That box? Oh, yes, I remember now. That box belonged to me. I often keep spare cash in the safe."

Both men looked at the safe facing them cemented into the wall of the manager's sitting-room.

"And the green and white striped paper? I showed the clerk the piece I found in this room the morning after Mr. Beale's—ah—departure, and he positively identifies it as similar to that which he saw in the safe. Yet when I questioned you, sir, about that same piece you expressly stated that it was not yours?"

The manager did not speak. He looked as if he could not, and after waiting a full minute the Chief Inspector rose.

"You have no explanation to offer, sir?"

"What do you mean?" snapped the manager shrilly. "I have explained! Good God, I am explaining! I may have wrapped a box up in any chance piece of paper I found lying around without noticing its colour —its stripes!"

Pointer waited again. Then:

"You have nothing further to add, sir?"

"No!" The manager passed his hand across his face as though to wipe away an incautious word.

The Chief Inspector took out a small black book from an inner pocket and held it in front of the other. "Do you identify this, sir?"

The manager's face glistened under the light.

"Of course. It's the safe receipt-book. You have no business with that, officer. Aren't you overstepping your authority?"

"I think not, sir. Here are the entries up to July 25th—the date Mr. Eames came to the hotel. Here are the entries up to August 4th, the date of his death —and here are the entries from August 4th up to date. Does nothing strike you about them?"

"Nothing!" The manager's voice was harsh. "They are all in perfect order. Each entry initialled by me and by the visitor, and the dated signed receipt in full when the article or articles were handed back. What mare's nest have you got hold of now?"

"You have no explanation to offer of the curious fact that up to the 25 th the entries are in a different ink from the receipts, and the receipts themselves differ according to the pen used. But from the twenty-fifth of July to August fourth inclusive, that is these ten pages"— he held them up—"though the handwriting differs as before, all the writing is done with one ink throughout and with one nib—a rather pointed fountain pen? After August fourth again the nibs and the ink varies as they do before July 25th.

"What do you mean?" The manager stared truculently at his inquisitor. "What are you insinuating?"

"Then, too," continued the detective's level tones, "this

book is one of a class Straker habitually stock. But this one is twenty pages short. Someone has evidently cut out the pages on which were the entries of July twenty-fifth to August fourth, and the half-pages which correspond further on, and filled in more or less complete copies— more or *less* complete"—he repeated meaningly—"of the pages as they stood."

There was a long silence.

"Here is a copy of the book, sir, but this one I am taking with me, as you have no explanations to offer."

The manager made a gesture towards the door and turned on his heel.

Saluting stiffly, Pointer left the room, and after a word to an unobtrusive figure watching outside, swung himself on to a Bayswater bus.

O'Connor received the news of the day's work with enthusiasm. The police officer took a more moderate tone and pointed out that they were only now where most cases started—that is, in possession of the name of the victim.

"—but I'm not denying it's a step forward, chiefly because it's our best chance of getting at the motive. And the motive will be the only key that will unlock this puzzle." He spoke with conviction. "If it were a case of circumstantial evidence we might spend the rest of our lives working at it. That balcony, that service-stair practically throw the case open to all London."

"What about Miss Leslie?"

The other stared a moment. "Well, what about her? Her alibi is fairly good. May be true, what young 'what's his name' says."

"You think it's the manager?"

"I wonder if I really do?" murmured Pointer sarcastically.

"Looks as though he were certainly in it for something, even if it's only shielding Beale," O'Connor answered for him. "Then there's Carter-Cox. He has a direct inducement."

"Very direct."

"Curious will that!" O'Connor spoke almost to himself.

"But then the whole thing is odd." Pointer puffed away in silence.

"True for you," O'Connor nodded; "the separate slips—that will sent to his old family solicitor, with whom he had had next to no dealings. And then you spoke of his clothes—"

"They struck even the jeweller when he went about his watch," agreed Pointer. "All well enough in their way, but not at all those of a wealthy young man."

"And a mother with over seven thousand a year, and an uncle worth as much, too—he must have made the money fly!"

O'Connor's tone of virtuous horror made Pointer think of Russell.

The next day was a Sunday, but the Chief Inspector arranged that Russell should send off a wire to Mrs. Erskine breaking the news to her that an accident had happened to Robert in London, followed by another telling her that the accident had been fatal. By the afternoon they had the reply from Nice: "Starting at once. Erskine." On Monday morning, however, came another cable from Mrs. Erskine, this time from Paris: "Ill. Doctor forbids journey." It was sent from the Gare St. Lazare station. Mr. Russell and Pointer set out the same day for the French capital. It was to Mr. Russell, naturally, that the task of telling the mother the facts about her son's death fell. In any case Pointer would have seen to it that the man who knew only the general outline should be the tale bearer. He saw no good in harrowing Mrs. Erskine's feelings prematurely with an account of the wardrobe and the police certainty of foul play.

He walked about Paris the morning after his arrival, wondering, as so often before, at the city's reputation for beauty. Charming in parts, yes, but—to his mind —its general reputation rested on "mass suggestion," so unspeakably dreary and sordid did he always find the greater part of it. The cafes with their comfortless chairs and tables at which people drank weirdly coloured drinks, of which—still according to him—the less said the better, were a back number compared with a London tea-room. He was glad when eleven struck, and he was shown into Mrs. Erskine's great bedroom. A thin figure, almost lost among her pillows on the couch, held out a trembling hand. Its chill told him how greatly Russell's story had drained the mother's vitality. He murmured some words of regret as he took a chair. The son had evidently inherited his mother's general air of pallor, and he saw where the young man had got his one peaked eyebrow from. The Abercrombie eyebrow, as Mr. Russell had called it. Mrs. Erskine had it very markedly, and its unlikeness to its fellow lifted her pale face out of the commonplace.

"Mr. Russell has just told me"—her voice was rather flat and toneless,—"all the details. I can't quite grasp what has happened yet, my only child. . . ."

Again he murmured a sentence of sympathy. "I wouldn't dream of intruding, madame," he said earnestly, "but we want to clear up the motives for what has happened. Had Mr. Robert Erskine ever spoken of putting an end to his life before?"

Mrs. Erskine did not answer for a moment or two. When she did it was with a visible effort. The Chief Inspector guessed what it must cost an evidently reserved woman to lay bare her lack of any affection from her son. "Not exactly . . . but my unhappy son did not find in life all he hoped from it, I fear. He liked gaiety—as youth always does,—and perhaps . . . life disappointed him. His letters—he wrote infrequently, naturally, his very popularity left him little time for writing—his letters seemed to me to show but little real happiness."

"Ah! his letters! May I see them?"

"Oh, I couldn't! My son's letters to me? Oh, no!" She shook her head resolutely, but he insisted, pointing out in his kindest way that the matter could not rest where it was, that some motive must have lain behind that draught of morphia, and that the letters might furnish the explanation. All of which was strictly true. Mrs. Erskine looked at him tragically.

"I cannot do it! I canna!" she whispered brokenly, but finally he persuaded her to draw out from under her cushion a leather pocket-book.

"Don't—don't misjudge him," she pleaded earnestly, looking away. "He was a good son and loved me, but it's not easy for a lad to put his love into words, is it?"

Certainly Robert Erskine had made but little effort in that direction. The letters were only those of the current year, with the exception of his last Christmas letter. Each was the barest of prefaces to a demand for money to pay some pressing debt. In one he apparently half-shamefacedly had added that the devil only knew where all his own money went to. In another, evidently in answer to some suggestion of his mother about living with an object in view, was a caustic line as to the differing estimates put on objects by an old lady and a young man; as for himself, he added candidly, it was to "squeeze the most out of this rotten show."

As a light on his character the four were damning in their clearness, and in so far they gave the Chief Inspector a very good idea of the vicious circle in which Robert Erskine must have lived; but they mentioned no names and no facts. Not even an address was given. The mother was directed to send the sums asked for, and very big sums they totalled all together, to the Toronto main postoffice. There was never a date or heading, but the Toronto post-mark on the envelopes supplied some clue. Of coming to Europe there was no word. It looked much as though young Robert's journey might easily have been a flight from unpleasant consequences, for Pointer knew, none better, where such paths as these could lead. He handed back the letters without a word, except of thanks. Mrs. Erskine covered her face with her hands and said nothing for a moment.

"You'll not—they don't do my poor lad justice—I shan't be called on to show them again?"

"No, no, madame!" Pointer was thankful that he need not turn the knife in a mother's wound. "No, there will be no necessity for any mention of them. But his other letters, now—?"

"I didn't keep them," she spoke in a low, pained voice, "you see, I never dreamt that they might be all that I should ever have— I always thought he would let me make my home with him some day—living alone is hard when your son is so far away—but that was not to be."

"You have no other letters from him, then?"

"None. I destroyed them each year. I make a practice of never keeping letters long. My health is none too certain."

"Did he ever refer to a John Carter in them?"

"You mean the John Carter to whom he left his money? Mr. Russell asked me about him, too. No, I never knew him mention any names or places to me."

"You know nothing of a man called Beale?"

"Nothing whatever."

Clearly it was no use putting any questions to her as to Robert's political views. "Before I leave, could you tell me how much his uncle left him?"

Mrs. Erskine sat silent awhile, evidently thinking deeply. She seemed a very accurate person. "He did say how much it was, but I forget the exact figures. I know he conveyed the impression that"—she bit her lip—"well, that the ball of life was now at his feet. My dear husband always spoke of Ian as a wealthier man than himself, but more than that I can't say."

It was a most painful interview. Pointer was thankful when he could close the door gently behind him with a gesture symbolical of his respectful pity.

Watts met him at Victoria Station, late though it was. The detective was eager to wipe out the memory of Mr. Russell's visit to the hotel room.

"I came across an interesting bit of evidence

yesterday, sir," he began as soon as they were in the taxi,
"in the manager's room. You know that steel locked box in
his desk? Well, he left his keys on his desk for a moment.
I slipped out of his bedroom, where I was keeping an eye
on him in accordance with your instructions, and
unlocked it. He rushed back a second later, picked up his
keys, and hurried off. I opened the box. There was
nothing in it but a new cheque book for the Chiswick
branch of the Midland bank with one cheque gone. It was
a close shave, for I had hardly laid it back in the box and
put it away again in its drawer when he came back and
went on with his writing. It was an order for some
repairs. I slipped out and down to Chiswick, and there I
had a bit of luck. Their doorkeeper is Higgins of the City
Police. He and I used to be on the same beat. So I showed
him the manager's photo, and had a chat with him. He
said the manager gave the name of Parsons, and called at
the bank to open an account. Higgins has been at the
branch for fourteen years, so he has the run of the place,
and during the lunch hour he managed to get a look at
the signature book. There was only one Parsons in it—T.
A. Parsons, of 8 Parma Crt., Turnham Green. He had
opened a current account on August 6, but the amount
Higgins couldn't find out. Off I went to the address. It's a
block of flats, and at No. 8 I asked for Mr. Parsons. It
seemed that on last Monday a Mr. Parsons had taken a
room which had been advertised as to let. The landlady
asked for payment in advance, so he paid for a week as
requested, and called daily for letters, saying that as his
mother was ill he might not move in till later in the week.
She had not seen him since Thursday, when he had left a
note saying that he was giving up the room, as his
mother's illness was taking a turn for the worse. I showed
her the manager's picture, which she and the servant
identified as Mr. Parsons. I pretended to be from his
bank, and said that there was some difficulty about a
pass book I had sent him which he had not received. Did
she know his home address? She did not. But both she

and the slavey were certain that a thick, sealed envelope, such as generally contains a pass book, had arrived, with the bank's name on the seals, on the morning when Mr. Parsons had left. That's all, sir."

"Good work, Watts, though, of course, it won't prove anything. A hotel manager will have a dozen excuses for a separate account, even under an assumed name, but still—it all fits in—perhaps too well. At any rate, it shows us what first class men we have trailing him."

"It's Marsh and Ketteridge, sir: they're both sharp fellows; but they say that the manager goes to his club and vanishes, or to some shop they've never heard of, which turns out to have a dozen entrances. Oh, he's clever enough!" They had arrived at Pointer's rooms, but he had Watts follow him in and share a supper.

"What changes at the hotel itself?"

"Two of the first floor rooms have fresh occupants. Mrs. Willett is still staying on. Miss Leslie is in bed with a bad cold."

"Nothing odd noticed?" Pointer asked the routine questions.

"Nothing reported by Miller, sir."

Only when the men had finished an excellent meal of gravy soup and fried chicken did Pointer hold out his hand for any cables from the Canadian police.

There were two. The first one ran:

"Toronto. John Carter, assistant manager of the Amalgamated Silk Mills of this town. Served in the war. Promoted Sergeant. Had local reputation of trustworthy man, but disappeared July fifteenth, together with Manager Robert Erskine. Warrant out for both men issued July eighteenth for embezzlement of the Amalgamated's funds."

This was quite along the lines Pointer had expected. He opened the second. It ran:

"Robert Erskine, Scotsman. Came Toronto seven years ago from Calgary as Manager of Amalgamated Silk Mills. Invested twenty thousand in Mills. Did well at first. Gone downhill since war. In hands of money-lenders. Disappeared June fifteenth, together with Assistant Manager John Carter. Warrant issued June eighteenth against both men for embezzlement of the Amalgamated's funds to amount not yet ascertained."

Both cables were signed by the Toronto Police Commissioner.

Watts had already seen them when the Assistant Commissioner at the Yard had sent them in. As no comment was made he ventured on one himself. "It looks very bad for the partner Cox, or Carter, doesn't it, sir?"

Pointer looked at him with the filmy eyes of deep thought. "Think so? Possibly."

"What do you think, Mr. O'Connor?"

O'Connor was quite willing to oblige. "Carter is a big chap by all accounts, and Erskine's friend. Why should he choose a place so certain to be discovered as a hotel bedroom? Why not take Erskine for a run in a motor, stun him, and drop him into a pond? I can't think he's such a fool as not to have been able to make some better opportunity than that wardrobe."

"Fit of passion, sir?"

"But," objected O'Connor, "why the marks of tugging on Erskine's collar which the photo shows?"

When Watts had taken a belated departure, O'Connor looked at his friend.

"So they're crooks. I shouldn't have thought that somehow. Your account of the honest marks of wear on Erskine's wardrobe made me put him down as poor but honest."

Pointer only smoked on, his hands clasped behind his neck.

"D'ye think some of your light-fingered friends have welcomed their brethren from across the ocean and the lot have fallen out?"

"This doesn't look like the work of anyone I can call to mind at the moment." Pointer ruminated over the masterpieces he had come across in the past. "Still you never know," he wound up.

During the night a cable from Calgary arrived and was duly waiting on his table at the Yard.

"Calgary. Robert Erskine, Scotsman. Inherited largest ranch here, Four Winds by name, from his uncle, Ian Erskine, twelve years ago. Sold it seven years ago at a loss and moved to Toronto. Reputation of uncle and nephew of the best in every way."

"John Carter. Frequent visitor at Four Winds. Prospector and son of a Toronto Prospector. Good repute."

Pointer meditated some time over this before he filed it. Another cable was sent to Toronto asking for full particulars of the warrant out against the two men, and the photos of both were duly posted for identification.

Mr. Russell dropped in on the Chief Inspector at lunch, but beyond a question as to whether he had ever heard that Robert Erskine was interested in any business Pointer kept his own counsel. The solicitor was evidently unaware that young Erskine did not still own the ranch.

"So you didn't get anything helpful by coming to Paris?" the solicitor continued, as the two men turned in for a cup of tea. He himself had been prostrated by the rough crossing the night before, and had hardly been able to exchange a couple of words with his companion in the crowded railway carriage.

"Except a general idea of the deceased's character as shown in his letters."

"Ah, yes, true. I had a long conversation with Mrs. Erskine and a very trying one."

"How so trying?"

"Aye, women, even the best of them shouldn't be

trusted with money."

The Scotsman drank his tea sternly. "She wants everything sold out and put into an annuity."

"She" of course referred to Mrs. Erskine. The Chief Inspector turned the matter over carefully to see whether he could extract any grist for his mills from it.

"Well, why not?"

"Eh, man, why not?" Then light seemed to break on the Scotsman. "Ah, I see I hadn't made myself clear. The trouble is, she wants it done immediately. You know how securities change. All of hers are good enough. Some very sound, some industrials. For instance, she put quite a large sum into some shares a few years ago which stood at twice what they stand at today. We approved after a fashion, provided she was willing to discount market fluctuations. But now she wants to fling some thousands of shares suddenly on the market—it's madness. The same way with some mortgages we arranged for her, you can't change that class of security into cash at a moment's notice. Yet that's what she wants. Of course, we won't do it. In her own interests we can't. I didn't tell her that naturally, but she'll find that it takes more time than she thinks to put a fortune as large as her half is into an annuity."

"I wonder why the hurry?" Pointer was deeply interested.

"I can't make it out." Mr. Russell's curiosity was evidently at work. "Mrs. Erskine has hitherto been such a good business woman. I'm the last to deny that she has made most advantageous purchases at times, but now to be willing to throw away at least one quarter of her fortune, if not a half, just for some mad whim of speed— it's beyond me. And an annuity, too! They're none so safe these days. Why not Government gilt-edged stocks? That's what I've been recommending to her, but no! It's to be an annuity and damn the cost. Man, I'm fairly tired out with yesterday's argybargy."

Pointer turned the whim of Mrs. Erskine over and

over in his mind while the inquest progressed next day, and finally laid the matter on one side, "to come up if called upon to do so" at some future time when it might fit some fresh fact.

The inquest caused a great stir among the papers, as any whisper of a murder always does, and in the facts as laid before the public—in a strictly limited dose —there was enough and to spare of the strange. Mr. Beale was not mentioned, neither was Mrs. Erskine, nor were the cables from Canada read, but a detailed account of the finding of the body by the police in the wardrobe, and of its belated identification, caused the evening papers to do a roaring trade, while the inquest itself was adjourned for another fortnight so as to "allow of the authorities in Canada being communicated with."

CHAPTER SIX

The very morning after the inquest a piece of news reached London that made the Chief Inspector jump for his hat. A wealthy American named Beale had been found bound and gagged in one of the leading Brussels hotels. The room where he was discovered belonged to another American named Green. Mr. Beale, on his release, had described to the reporters how he had been lured to the room under the pretext of purchasing a rare painting, robbed, and left tied up and gagged. The description of his assailant tallied with the man wanted by the Yard as Cox, or Carter. Pointer flew across within a couple of hours after opening his morning paper, and found Mr. Beale surrounded by a knot of reporters. Beale looked up at him with a saturnine grin.

"Yes, it's me, Chief. I'm too young and inexperienced for this wicked world. Have a drink?" The American dismissed the reporters good-naturedly but firmly. Then he smiled, showing his teeth in an apparent merriment which never touched his eyes—cold and keen.

"Well, I guess I'll come across with the story. That man who called himself Green is one of our cleverest crooks. He certainly doesn't live up to his name! I was after him in London when I stumbled into that queer story of Eames. Oh, I'm on my vacation all right, but there's no holiday that would do me the good that getting my hands on Green would. Personal reasons— always the toughest, eh, Chief?"

Evidently Mr. Beale had not yet had time to read the London news, for the "Eames Case" had now become the "Erskine Murder."

"By the way"—again came that swift baring of the teeth—"you haven't asked me yet"—he underscored the "yet" with a glance—"how I came to run away from the Enterprise without saying good-bye to anyone. Well, I'll tell you. I had just got up from my cosy armchair and made a start for bed when who should pass the window— I had opened it—but Green. Yes, Green, the man my paper had tried so hard to get in N'York and fallen flat over. He had an overcoat on his arm, and his grip in his hand, so I just whipped out of the window and followed him to a garage. Went in after him and arranged for a faster car than his little two-seater. Picked up his trail without any effort, for he had hired the machine and driver in Dover, and the man was to drive him back for the boat. I did the same. We crossed together, and I followed him here to Brussels. He doesn't know me by sight, so I laid what I thought

was a first class trap for him. Everything went according to plan—except the end." He made a grimace. "Behold me minus the crook, my diamond ring, my pocket-book and my reputation for brains, to say nothing of my night's sleep. You see, Green knew all the time who I was, and I'm bound to say he's a hustler."

"Why do you call him Green?" asked Pointer slowly.

"Why shouldn't I? It's as much his name as any of the others he uses, I guess."

"What others, for instance?"

"Well-1,—Shepherd, Smith, are two others."

"What about Cox, or Carter?"

Just for a second Pointer saw a contraction of the American's pupils.

"Carter? Cox? Do you know him, too, at Scotland Yard?"

"Mr. Beale, may I ask you for the fullest possible details of the man you call Green?"

"Better search our police files. A cleverer criminal doesn't snap his fingers at our detectives."

"Any murders to his name?"

"Well-1, I don't know about murders, but for robbery with or without violence he's a master."

"Will you describe him, sir?"

"My language might pain you, Chief, but here's the police docket of him from N'York." He handed the Chief Inspector a typewritten numbered slip, which described one Henry Green, alias Arthur Shepherd, alias—The description tallied exactly with the man Carter. The snapshot appended was that of a clever face, full of daring and with a resolute chin. The specimen hand- writing was that familiar to Pointer both from the Hotel Marvel and from the register below in the Lion Blanc.

He studied the slip very carefully. He noted that Carter, or Green, had never yet been actually captured or stood his trial. All the evidence against him seemed to be held back in the police hands.

"You can keep that if you like, Chief."

"Thank you, sir. That's a great help. And now, sir, what made you choose the Enterprise Hotel in the first place?"

"I had information that Green had been seen a couple of days before going in there. Mistaken information, I guess. The fool mixed it up with another hotel lower down."

"You had never seen Eames before?"

"*Eames?* Never. My reason for suspecting that something was wrong in the room was exactly what I told you."

He looked the police-officer squarely in the eye. Pointer had received excellent witness of Mr. Beale's character and reputation, and yet—he was sure that the other had recognised the corpse. He decided to blurt out Eames' real name. "We have found out that Eames was really a Scotsman named Erskine living in Canada; and to the best of our belief the man you call Green, and speak of as a well-known crook who goes under many aliases, is his partner, John Carter. Both are wanted for embezzlement, we are told, though so far no particulars have come in."

Mr. Beale looked the picture of surprise.

"You don't say!" There was a short pause. Pointer wondered whether Mr. Beale was choosing his next words with care.

"Partner in what? Safe-opening? What kind of a business did this Eames, I forget what you called him, run?"

"We hear that he was manager of the Toronto Silk Mills."

Mr. Beale made no comment except to give a cluck of amazement. There was a little pause, then the Englishman came back to the case in hand.

"May I ask, sir, why you didn't write and let us know where you were? Your evidence was greatly wanted at the last inquest, and will be absolutely necessary in two weeks' time."

Mr. Beale raised his eyebrows. "It may be quite impossible for me to come over," he said coldly; "and as to writing—the American Embassy was informed of my whereabouts, I guess."

The police-officer rose.

"Then, sir, if I can be of no use here, I wish you a good-morning," he began formally; but Mr. Beale, having shown his superiority to any police regulations, pressed him down into his chair with an affable hand, and this time insisted on ordering a drink. Pointer chose tea, which seemed to the other originality verging on eccentricity, and took his leave as soon as he could escape. He made no mention of the green and white striped paper. Mr. Beale was not the kind of man of whom to ask too many explanations, but the Chief Inspector was closeted for some time with a Brussels *confrere,* and if the Belgium police were openly to hunt for the missing Green, the Yard received the private assurance that they would also not forget to keep an unobtrusive eye on the wealthy, well-documented Mr. Beale, who still puzzled Pointer. That astute officer never for a moment forgot the sketchy alibi, the cigar ashes over Erskine's tie, the emptied basin, and various other puzzling odds and ends, such as the scrap of green and white wrapping paper picked up in a room where he had spent many hours. It was still Mr. Beale who struck Pointer as not fitting into the picture. He thought that the American's presence gave an unreal effect. That where he showed, an impartial scrutiny could dimly detect different outlines and other colours beneath.

The adjourned inquest was duly held. Mr. Beale did not appear, but the evidence against Carter, alias Cox, was given by Pointer and Watts, as well as by the Enterprise manager and employees. Carter's photograph was identified by the Marvel Hotel as that of Cox. There was the motive as shown in Erskine's will, the purchase by him of the medicine—the vehicle in which the poison was given—there was Carter's flight and silence, and, lastly, his desperate effort in Brussels to throw any pursuer off his track. There were the mud marks on the balcony, and the wax vestas.

A verdict was brought in against the Canadian for the murder of his partner, and his portrait was published in the papers, so that all honest men could be on the watch for him. But Pointer was not satisfied.

"I wonder if the whole investigation is on the wrong line—whether the points have been missed somewhere, but where?" He asked O'Connor, who only shook his head in silence, and left his friend to sit up smoking and thinking long after he himself had gone to bed.

From the Brussels police came the news that they had not been able to discover any trace of Green, but that Beale had gone to Lille, and so was out of their jurisdiction. Watts was despatched post-haste to the French town to pick up the American's trail, but before he came on it a wire reached Pointer from the Editor himself.

"Located Green-Carter. Come immediately."

Pointer crossed that night. He had a little talk with a

Frenchman in plain clothes who seemed to be expecting him at the station before Lille, and, descending on the platform of that prosperous town, was met by the impatient Mr. Beale and by Watts.

"I thought you would never get here. Train's an hour late. He's staying in a room in the Rue Sentier near here under the name of Thompson. He's out just now, and we can wait for him there. The maid thinks I'm a friend of his."

The Chief Inspector nodded briefly and followed Mr. Beale to a corner shop in a quiet street. A side entrance took them up a flight of stairs to the first floor. Here beside the door of a flat was another smaller one.

"That's his room." Mr. Beale rang the bell of the larger door.

A French woman opened. Mr. Beale asked for his friend. Mr. Thompson was out again, he was informed, but he would be in shortly. If messieurs his friends cared to wait she would unlock the door for them. She smilingly inserted a key. Pointer thought that the American made as if to shut the door behind him a trifle quickly, but the maid came on into the room and altered a chair.

"*Tiens!* Mr. Thompson is leaving us? Ah, no; there is his trunk. It is only his hand-bag that has gone." And she left them alone.

"Want to examine the trunk?" asked the American. "I suppose your warrant justifies that?"

"Quite. Funny about the bag, isn't it?"

"That's what startled me. We don't want to slip up on him again."

Pointer thought that Mr. Beale had looked annoyed rather than startled by the maid's question. He himself walked slowly around the room. Watts had been left on duty below. He looked at a box of vestas on the mantelpiece. They were the same as those found in No. 14 of the Enterprise. Certainly for an expert crook the room was strangely bare.

A step sounded on the stairs. Mr. Beale jumped

behind the door, ready to close it. The police-officer seated himself facing the door. A key was inserted, the door was flung widely open, and a young man with a couple of heavy parcels in his arms entered with a decided limp, but swung the door shut with one agile foot. It was the face Pointer had seen photographed as Green. A resolute, strong face, set on a powerful rangy frame.

He caught sight of the impassive figure by the table with the steady eyes fixed on him and stopped. For a second he stood staring, a curious grey creeping under his tan.

"I'm not alone, Mr. Carter, and even if I were, violence wouldn't help you," said the Chief Inspector, rising to his feet. He knew what that tightened jaw meant. "I have a warrant here for your arrest charging you with the murder of Robert Erskine in London on August 4. Of course, as you know, if you wish it I must call in the French authorities; but the end will be the same. It will save time if you come quietly with me back to England and let me arrest you at Dover. I must warn you that anything you say may be used in evidence against you."

The young man made no reply; his eyes were now fixed on the table. He was evidently thinking hard. A bead of sweat trickled down his temple.

"A French prison is very uncomfortable, but please yourself." Pointer hoped the young man would take it sensibly.

Carter—to give him the name under which his warrant had been issued—looked around the room. A flash came into his eyes as he caught sight of Mr. Beale bolting the door.

"Pity I didn't kill you when I had the chance!" he spat out between clenched teeth.

Mr. Beale looked pointedly at the police-officer.

"You had better take it quietly. Talk of that kind won't help your case," that official warned, phlegmatically.

Carter sat down.

"May I smoke?"

"A cigarette of mine, or here's my pouch if you'll let me have a look at your pipe first." Pointer looked through the bowl and handed his briar back to Carter, who filled it, and then, hunching his shoulders, puffed away with his feet stuck straight out in front of him, his eyes on his boots. The Chief Inspector looked at him keenly. The man really was engrossed in calculations of some kind. Concentration oozed from him. The police-officer was on the alert. He had seen something like this once before, when a man had been arrested on a capital charge, and the result had been a swift suicide.

"It's a pretty average frowst in here; can the window be opened?"

Pointer flung it open and stood squarely in the opening.

Carter gave a harsh laugh, like a bark.

"Suicide? Me? Not on your life!"

The other did not move away. "Well?" he asked. "Do you want an extradition order?"

"I'll come. Got to. Handcuffs, I suppose?" His voice was suddenly weary.

Pointer did not reply. He never permitted himself to have any emotion towards a prisoner, but he felt sure that O'Connor would have been sorry for the chap in front of him. He cut the strings of the package on the table. Mr. Beale pressed forward.

"Ah, ha! Electrical plant. Something new in the safe-breaking line, eh, Green?"

Carter bared two rows of strong teeth. He did not look pleasant. The Englishman was conscious of an undertone as of a secret duel going on. Was it merely that the Editor had run the criminal to earth, who for so long had evaded justice, and evidently on some occasion tricked him? He looked as keenly at Mr. Beale as at Carter. The Editor's eyes were alight with triumph. Carter watched him dully, looking years older than the young man who had flung the door open. He strolled over to the window, and

Pointer tensed himself, but Carter merely shot out a long, thin hand and pulled the curtain across the shut half.

Mr. Beale, with a wonderfully agile spring—all things considered—switched it back.

"No signalling to your accomplices, Green!"

Carter swore at him, and swore strongly.

"Come, come," the Chief Inspector interposed sternly, "none of that! Mr. Beale, may I trouble you to call up my man who's down below; and where would you like me to meet you afterwards?"

Mr. Beale gave a half-shrug.

"Considering that I put the case in your hands, Chief, instead of the French authorities, I think that I'm hardly being treated quite fairly. Surely there can be no objection to my being present at the search of the room. Remember I'm in a very responsible position."

"Quite so, sir, and I'm sure I'm much obliged to you," the other bowed, "but I'm afraid routine work has to be done as routine."

"I shall report what you say to the proper quarter." Mr. Beale spoke very quietly.

For a second Pointer hesitated. The case did owe Mr. Beale a tremendous lot. He had notified the finding of Erskine's dead body. In some equally mysterious way he had found the "wanted" man. But Pointer thought that the American's flair for discoveries betokened some private knowledge which might alter many obscurities if he would speak. So he contented himself with merely bowing.

Mr. Beale shot him one of his steely glances.

"I shall expect you at the depot," he said briefly. "I suppose you are taking the four twenty-five back." He strode off with as much dignity as his short stature allowed. On the whole, the police-officer was rather glad that he was annoyed, as he might be the less likely to notice the French detective to whom Pointer had spoken on his way in to Lille, and who was to follow the Editor's every step.

When the door closed, Carter flung a bunch of keys down on the table. "You've got the grip. I suppose you didn't find in it what you are all looking for? You won't find it in the trunk either." His tone was rough. His whole intonation had changed from that of a well-educated man to something coarser.

Pointer signed to Watts to open the trunk. Leaving him to guard the prisoner, the Chief Inspector himself searched it. One of the first things he picked up was a London telephone directory; after that came a list of Paris bankers. Just the literature to expect from a man of "Green's" reputation. He ran his fingers among the clothes. His practised tips encountered something in the lining of a coat. He drew it out, made a slit, and, inserting a finger, brought out a long string of pearls with an antique emerald fastening. He laid it beside him without a word. Carter had risen from his chair and was watching intently. When the pearls lay on the table he made a curious gesture with his hands, and, sinking back on to his chair, covered his face, which had turned livid. Pointer went on methodically. Several rings, a diamond necklace, and a jewelled pendant were discovered. Finally the trunk was turned upside down, and on the very bottom he pounced on a twist of newspaper. Inside were a few screws. The two officers examined them closely, then the Chief Inspector took out an envelope and fastened them carefully inside.

"Any explanation you wish to offer, Carter? I have cautioned you already?"

Carter shook his head.

The police finished their work, and in silence, arm in arm, like the best of friends, the three walked to the station in plenty of time to catch the Calais express. Pointer left Mr. Beale and Watts to sit beside Carter in the reserved compartment Mr. Beale had ordered, and went off to have a cup of coffee. A man selling postcards approached him and saluted with an odd little jerk. The Englishman glanced over his wares and picked out two.

"Can you put them in an envelope for me?"

"But yes, monsieur, but yes," and the man slipped the cards into one and passed on. Outside the cafe the Chief Inspector drew out a sheet of thin paper. It was a record of Mr. Beale's movements from the time he left Carter's room. "X went from Rue Sender to the post. Sent telegram to 'M. Garnier, Notaire, Rue Bizet, Geneve': 'Series accepted. Editor.' After that, X lounged the time away till he joined you at the station."

Pointer wired to Geneva for full particulars as to M. Garnier, and took his seat in the train. Carter would be tried first in London for the murder of Erskine, and, if acquitted, would be sent to Canada to stand his trial there for embezzlement and, doubtless, robbery. The young man seemed quite conscious of his position. For the most part he sat with his eyes closed, only the tense look of his jaw and the pulse hammering in his temples showing that he was not asleep. As for Mr. Beale, Pointer would have gladly dispensed with his company, for there was a gloating triumph in the American's whole attitude which seemed to the police-officer positively indecent.

Back at the Yard, where he reported at once to the Assistant-Commissioner, he found a cable identifying the photographs of both Robert Erskine and John Carter as that of the two men, respectively, who were wanted under a warrant taken out in New York by the President of the Amalgamated Silk Mills, a huge concern which practically held a monopoly of the silk spinning and weaving industry. Defalcations extending over many years were spoken of, and cooked balance-sheets, but up to the present the exact amount supposed to have been taken by the Toronto manager and his assistant was not known.

The Chief Inspector filed the information, and made his way to his rooms, where, as he hoped, he found another cable, a private one from a friend of his in the Canadian police. It was in answer to a long cable from himself asking him to find out all he could about the

warrant for Erskine and Carter. Pointer raised his eyes
at its length. Wright was absolutely reckless of expense
when he wanted to be clear. The cable read:

*"We must stand well with Yank police because of
coming Burton affair. Warrant issued New York on
Heilbronner's sworn deposition. Heilbronner millionaire
chairman of Amalg. Spotty reputation. Warrant gives no
facts. Can. police passive. If Carter arrested by Yanks or
you, and sent here, proofs of defalcations, etc., will be
demanded before Can. police hand him over."*

The Burton affair, as Pointer knew, concerned a
murderer who had escaped into the United States and
was very much "wanted" in his home. So, like the
robberies in which Carter, as Green, was supposed to be
implicated, there were no actual proofs of embezzlement
made public. Pointer had very little to say that night even
to O'Connor, and early next morning visited Carter in his
cell. The Canadian had refused as yet to see a lawyer.
The long vacation was on, and his case could not come up
till the autumn. He seemed sunk in depression. And the
case against him was certainly black enough. The screws
found in his trunk were the mates of those which fixed
the screwed-on panels to the wardrobe. He gave no
explanation of them. He gave no explanation of anything,
not even of the jewellery, which was to be identified by a
couple of American detectives who were coming over on
purpose. The Heads at the Yard were quite certain of his
guilt on both counts, murder and theft, but the Chief
Inspector said as little as possible. He had asked the
Canadian to at least help him to trace what might have
been wrapped up by Erskine in that strip of green and
white paper, but after a second's flash of hope in the
accused's sombre eyes he had shaken his head and
refused to speak.

Pointer had no sympathy whatever with this kind of
an attitude. He considered it not fair to the accused and

not fair to the police. It was all very well for his superiors to be so certain of Carter's guilt. When the case came up for trial it was he and not they who would have to pay for any mistake, and apart from this personal consideration, the Chief Inspector had a high standard of fair play, and the idea that he might be a party to injustice was intolerable to him. Not that he by any means thought Carter innocent. As the Canadian would not give any alibi, he apparently had had the opportunity to commit the murder. The will was considered to be an additional motive, besides wanting to get rid of an inconvenient accomplice, but what had Erskine to leave? Mr. Russell had not been able to trace any "available" funds. Yet the dead man would hardly have alluded to a stolen hoard without giving any indications as to where such a hoard might be found.

"And where does Beale come in, and what of the manager, whose back garden you've been digging up so carefully?" O'Connor demanded rhetorically one night, after enduring his friend's silence as long as he could.

"The manager—humph! Mr. Beale?—He certainly must have a very strong feeling against Carter. Yet he looks the last man to let his feelings alone carry him very far. And why is he so keen on seeing Carter? He makes every sort of an effort to get an order. I think he was amazed when he found out that even a letter from his ambassador wouldn't be of any use if Carter refused to see him, and refuse he does. You know, O'Connor, I'd give a good deal to place Mr. Beale in all this."

"You surprise me!" murmured the Irishman sarcastically.

"What gain is it of his if Carter is hung or locked up in gaol? I've tried to get to the bottom of his game —for that he's playing one I'm still as certain as ever, but I can't find a hook to hang anything on. I've had report after report about him from America. He seems to be beyond suspicion. He is on the board of that Silk Company which owned Erskine's Toronto Mills, but that doesn't throw any light on his feeling towards Carter."

"Didn't he say that he had his knife into him because of some family jewels Carter had stolen?"

"He did. Mr. Beale always has an explanation for anything. Why doesn't he write to Carter if he's so keen on seeing him? He won't. Of course, he may be quite straight in all this. That telegram of his to Geneva, now— the man he sent it to is one of the most respected solicitors in the town. I've absolutely nothing to go on"

"What about Watts' idea that the crime might be political?"

Pointer shook his head. "Not a shred of evidence to bear that out. Quite the other way. Well, I'm thinking of taking my holiday, which is due this month, abroad. I shouldn't wonder if it led me to Geneva and home by way of Nice."

"Do you think you could pick up anything there?"

"Doubtful. Still, I like to cover the whole ground."

But before the time for Pointer's well-earned leave, on an early evening in September his landlady announced a young lady to see him.

The Chief Inspector laid down his pipe. O'Connor was away, and he wheeled up his friend's capacious armchair for his caller.

An exceedingly good-looking, well-dressed young woman entered. Undoubtedly a lady, and yet to his keen eyes with a something about her he found difficult to place.

"Chief Inspector Pointer?" Her accent told him what it was that had puzzled him. She was from the other side of the ocean. He bowed in his most friendly manner, and pulled O'Connor's chair still more into the light. She sank into it, and gave him the longest, keenest look the police-officer had ever had from a woman. Obviously she was weighing him carefully. Then she smiled.

"I'm glad I came. I made the manager of the Enterprise Hotel give me your private address. My name is Christine West; I'm a sort of adopted niece of Mr. Ian

Erskine of Calgary. Here is my passport, and here is a letter with another photo in it of mine from the Head of the Toronto police. I got him to certify that I really am Miss West."

The Chief Inspector was even more on the alert than before, if possible, when he handed her back her papers and photographs.

"Uncle Ian was a bachelor, you know, and my mother kept house for him after father died. That was twenty-three years ago, and Four Winds was my home till Uncle Ian's death. A dear and happy home it was, too." Her eyes grew soft. "I saw about poor Rob's death in the papers a little over a month ago, and about John Carter's arrest. My mother is dead, so I'm my own mistress, and I set out right away to see what can be done. For something has got to be done."

CHAPTER SEVEN

Miss West looked at the man sitting at his ease on the other side of the fireplace with a very determined tilt of her chin.

"Now, Mr. Pointer—you mustn't mind if I call you that, but I'm not talking to the Inspector of Scotland Yard just now—"

"*A* Chief Inspector from the Yard—" he corrected modestly, disclaiming the elevated rank she thrust upon him.

"I don't want to see *him*. I want a talk with just Mr. Pointer—a man,—a human being—who can be sorry for folk in trouble, and not look on them just as cases."

"But you see . . ." Pointer's face was very kind . . . "any information given to me is sure to be overheard by the Chief Inspector, and he may feel it his duty to make use of it. There's no use pretending he won't, miss."

She sat a moment studying him again.

"Very well. Let him overhear what he likes, but all the same I want to talk to you, and not to a police-officer. I want you, and not the Inspector, to talk the case over with me, or we shall never get anywhere. And that's just where the police are in this case."

"Eh? Where?"

"Nowhere!" Miss West's eyes snapped; "nowhere at all with John Carter in prison! Now, Mr. Pointer"—her smile was infectious—"you see my position, don't you? A police-officer doesn't have any personal opinions— how can he have? But you have, you know."

"Well?" Pointer was smiling.

Miss West jumped up and paced up and down the room. She walked with a fine, free swing.

"I'll start at the very beginning. John Carter's father"—Pointer noticed that Carter was to be more to the fore than Robert Erskine—"was a prospector. He and Uncle Ian became great friends out on a shooting expedition uncle took once, and after that Mr. Carter used to regularly stop at Four Winds on his way out and back from his trips. I don't remember him well. I was such a little tot at the time. He was a widower, and once, after Jack had been ill, Uncle Ian insisted on his sending him to stay at Four Winds for six months. After that Jack used to spend his holidays from school regularly with us, and when Uncle Henry—I call him that, though, of course, he wasn't any relation to me, any more than Uncle Ian was—well, when Uncle Henry and Rob came out from England we had great times together, we three. Jack was the eldest, he was fifteen; then came Rob, who was twelve, and then I, a year younger than Rob." She paused a moment, evidently back in the happy days of which she was speaking, then with a sigh she went on: "Jack's father died when he was about eighteen. He went to the Calgary College to study engineering, but of course he lived at Four Winds. Mr. Carter had died, leaving awfully little behind him. Uncle Ian would have paid Jack's college expenses, but he would have none of that. He used to work just like any one of the hands on the Ranch in his holidays, and took his pay just like them. Then before he was through college Uncle Ian died, Dear, kind, generous Uncle Ian! We found out that he was fearfully badly hit by some wheat speculations he had got into, which did well at first and then let him in for thousands. He had mortgaged the ranch up to the last fence rail, and though it all went to Rob, there was fearfully little money for him to carry on with. Well, of course, after uncle's death everything was different. I didn't see much of the boys at this time. Rob decided to sell the ranch. Mother moved to a sister of hers in Toronto, where I was studying, and after college I got a post in the High School there. Finally Rob put the money

from the ranch into the Silk Mills at Toronto and came on
there as their manager. He did well, too, and was quite
one of Toronto's smart young men. Then came the war."
She paused for a minute or two. "Jack enlisted in the
Princess Pats, and went out with the first draft; he was
frightfully injured at Vimy trying to get his officer back
from between the lines. He was in hospital in France for
months and then was invalided out, but he stayed on in
France till the armistice, giving engineering courses in
the Y.M.C.A., I believe."

"And Mr. Robert Erskine?"

"Rob didn't go out. The factory was turned into
surgical supplies, and he thought he could do as good
work there as in Europe. Besides, he had lost his heart to
a girl who was practically German, a Miss Heilbronner.
That was how he originally got his chance as manager of
the Silk Mills. Old man Heilbronner was the head of the
American syndicate which owned the Toronto factory and
mills."

"Was Mr. Erskine engaged to Miss Heilbronner?"

"For a time, just before and at the beginning of the
war, I think he was—sort of on probation, if he could keep
on making good. I saw her once or twice out motoring
with Rob, and she didn't look the kind to do life on the
cheap. Then something happened—I don't know what—
which seemed to come between Rob and the
Heilbronners. You see," she turned to the other, "mother
and aunt and I didn't belong in the least to Rob's real
people. I mean—well, of course, I called Uncle Ian 'uncle,'
but we were just plain farmer folk same as Jack Carter.
The Erskines were quite different, and though Rob never
changed an iota himself, his circle and mine didn't mix.
Well, Mattie Heilbronner got engaged to another man,
and old man Heilbronner was out to get Rob's scalp, so I
heard people say; and certainly the factory, which had
done so splendidly up till then, didn't seem to do so well
after the trouble, whatever it was. But Rob kept his end
up till after the armistice, when it was turned back into

silk weaving again. Then Jack came back from Europe, and he insisted on coming in to help Rob. Wouldn't take a cent except out of profits, and they thought they were going to pull through in spite of Heilbronner's millions against them. But things went from bad to worse. They were just being squeezed out, so folks that knew said, and—" She came to a dead stop.

"Mr. Pointer, I've read the dreadful things they say of Jack Carter in the papers here. Are they true? I mean, did you *really* find all those jewels in his trunk? You yourself? And does he still refuse to explain?"

Pointer was quite honest with her. He told her exactly what the papers knew, but he did not add that the American police claimed to know Carter as Green. She said nothing for a minute or two, but sat down in her chair again, propping her chin on her hand, looking out of the window. She took up her story as though she had not asked any question.

"And then on June nineteenth the Toronto papers were out in head-lines that both Rob and Jack had disappeared, and that a warrant was out for their arrest for embezzlement. And that's all I know."

"All?" asked Pointer very quietly.

She flushed.

"I had a letter from Jack and one from Rob sent me on June fifth from Toronto. Just a line—literally —to say good-bye and that I should hear from them again."

"Have you the letters?"

"No, they were each marked 'Burn,' and I did so at once."

"And—did you hear from either of them again?"

"Not a word. I saw Rob's death in the paper. I didn't recognise him in that picture as Eames, and then I—I read of Jack's dreadful trouble."

There was a long silence between the two.

"And Mr. Beale? Where does he come in?"

"Beale?" She repeated the name questioningly. "Who is he? Never heard the name that I know of."

"Humph! And Miss Heilbronner, what of her?"

"She married still another man, so someone told me, shortly after the armistice. But Mr. Pointer, you're thinking of Rob Erskine. I'm not. Not for the moment. It's John Carter we must save. Poor Rob is killed, but Jack—" There were tears in her eyes which she winked resolutely away. "Mr. Pointer, you're a fair-minded man, one only has to look at you to see you wouldn't have a hand in faking up a case against an innocent man, and the case against Jack *is* faked."

"Then why doesn't he speak out, Miss West?"

"I can't imagine. I can't imagine!" She spoke as one who had tried hard enough, "but he's no murderer, far less a thief."

Pointer was sorry for her, and stirred uneasily in his chair.

"You see, I knew him as a boy, and knew him as a young man. You can't make a mistake as to the very foundations of a character you've known so long and so intimately. Uncle Ian, too, loved him. He loved him better even than Rob, and Uncle Ian couldn't have cared for anyone who wasn't straight." Again there was a silence between the two. Then she leant forward and laid a hand on Pointer's sleeve for a second.

"Do *you* think he's in danger, too, Mr. Pointer?" she whispered.

"Unless he speaks out, and can clear himself with a good alibi, I do, indeed. I'm speaking only of the murder charge—the other doesn't concern us over here. Now, Miss West, you think the charge against Carter is faked. That means he must have a bitter enemy. Robert Erskine was murdered, not by Carter, you say. He, too, had a bitter enemy. Could the same enmity link the two? Can they have a common enemy? Do you know of any event in their lives, common to both, which could have roused any such feeling on the part of anyone?"

She sank into deep thought and then slowly shook her head.

"Of course, one's first thought is that they were partners together, disappeared together, and were accused together of embezzlement. Could Mr. Heilbronner be in it for anything?" probed the police-officer.

"Mr. Heilbronner has been touring Europe for his health since July. I heard by chance on the steamer I crossed on that he was staying in Geneva, but I can't think of him as caring for anything but his money-bags— at least judging by his looks."

"Humph, not always a safe guide. Now about his daughter. Was Mr. Carter a friend of hers, too?"

"No he never met her. That I know."

"And you can think of nothing, absolutely nothing, which will give us any clue as to an enmity for one or both of these two men?"

"The Amalgamated Silk Society—but that sounds too silly to suggest," she said hesitatingly.

"I don't know about silly, but as they wanted both men for embezzlement I can't see the point in killing one. And Miss West, you can't separate one man in this case from the other, since Carter won't speak out. It is the charge of killing Erskine that's Carter's danger. Now suppose you tell me more about Carter. We have been told by the authorities in Toronto that even though he was Erskine's assistant he would absent himself from the town and the works for months at a time. Can you guess why?"

"Rob said he was prospecting."

"And what did he himself say?"

"He refused to talk of where he had been."

"Miss West, why don't you believe that he really had been prospecting?"

For an appreciable second she hesitated, then with a lift of her head she looked up at him.

"I'll be quite frank. I *know* the truth can only help Jack in the end. He never came back looking in the least as a prospector does after a trip. Face and hands burnt and cracked. Hair all rough, and a gait that doesn't lose its stiffness for weeks. There's an unmistakable look about a man who's been away in the wilds that you can't mistake out there. But Jack always came back paler than he went, and with his hands not sunburnt in the least. Nor has he ever been able to walk much since the war. It was his leg that was so mangled."

Pointer thought of "Green's" New York record.

"Now once more about the breaking off of the engagement between Robert Erskine and Miss Heilbronner. I wish you'd tell me all you know about it."

"I never got to the bottom of it because Rob was too cut up to talk of it. Perhaps it was only that old man Heilbronner didn't think the mills were turning out enough money for his daughter. He tried his best to get the place away from Rob, but Rob wouldn't let it go. There was some sort of a clause by which he could purchase it, so much down at once and the rest yearly. He had paid the sum down out of the ranch sale, and I guess the old man was always hoping he'd trip up on his payments, but Rob held on for seven years in spite of all, and then they—he—failed on the last instalment. Oh, Mr. Pointer, it was cruel! He first, and then Jack with him, had worked so hard. They had done without everything, pleasures, or enough sleep, or even"—she choked—"enough food those last months, and they just slipped up on it. He needed five thousand pounds, and so, though it cut him to do it, he wrote to his mother for the loan of the money. She sent one thousand pounds and he couldn't scrape the rest of the money together, try as he could. No one in Toronto would give him any help. That was the doing of the Silk Amalgamated. So he lost the mills and they even tried to turn him and Jack out of their positions, but Rob and he refused to leave. And that"—she sprang to her feet again. "I'm sure that is the real reason for the charge of embezzlement—just to break Rob and Jack because they dared to stand out against the Amalgamated. Mr. Heilbronner swore that they had been cheating the company out of its percentages for three years. Said that the Amalgamated had proofs of big orders carried out at the Toronto Mills which weren't entered on the books and on which nothing had been paid."

Pointer tried here and there to come upon something approaching a clue, but finally he saw Miss West into a taxi, and promised to call upon her next morning. Then he sat up till far into the night trying to clear up the new tangles which she had introduced.

Why—among many other ways—had Erskine given no idea of the nature of his work to his mother? He had only written infrequently, but even so he never referred to it. He only asked for funds and wrote as an idle young man about town. Why had he told Miss West that he had asked for five thousand pounds, when Pointer had read his own letter asking for one thousand pounds exactly. Where had the rest of the money gone which the young man had asked for and received, at the rate of about two thousand a year? As yet Pointer had been able to find no proof that Erskine speculated, though had he done so under another name it would be difficult to trace it. However, the Chief Inspector went to bed with a clear plan as to how Miss West would work into his schemes.

When he saw her next morning the wily man began by regretting that there seemed no way in which she could make herself of actual service such as she wanted to be engaged on, and only when Miss West was in a sufficiently subdued frame of mind at the idea of not being able to help after all did he advance his suggestion.

"I hope you won't mind my asking," he began, "but is there any—eh—tie between you and Mr. Carter?"

"He won't let me consider myself engaged to him, but if ever he gets enough money to marry on, he and I are going to be married. I have a little income of my own, but he won't let that count." She gave a proud little smile.

"I see." Pointer looked reflectively at his gloves. "I see. I was wondering if there isn't some way we could use your offer of help, but there is only one and you might not care for that." He seemed to dismiss the idea. She leant forward eagerly.

"Oh, but I'll do anything. *Anything*. I would for Rob's sake, let alone in the terrible position Jack is in. What is it, Mr. Pointer?"

"Well, it's this. I wonder if you could go to France and look up Mrs. Erskine's circle? As a sort of relation, well then a friend of the family, her solicitor, Mr. Russell, would give you a letter of introduction, I know. If possible I should like you to stay in the house and try to find some clue which might clear up all this game of cross-purposes, for that's what's going on, Miss West. There's no one case so tangled as this. What's happened, I feel sure, is that half-a-dozen ends have all got knotted up together. Now the real one may lie in the far past—back of Robert Erskine, or even of his father. I can see no other way of possibly stumbling on it than by trying to piece it out of his mother's recollections. Mrs. Erskine thinks there's nothing to tell, Mr. Russell says the same, but it's the only chance for a fresh cast as far as I can see. Will you go?"

As he had foreseen, the idea did not appeal to Miss West in the least.

"You mean," she hesitated, "you mean to go and stay with Mrs. Erskine, if she will let me, and be a sort of spy in the house?"

"Just so. No, I was afraid it wouldn't do. As a matter of fact, I wish I could have had someone in her villa weeks ago. Only the Yard won't run to needless expenses, you know, and—well, there it is." He smiled cheerily.

"You think it so important as all that?"

He was quite honest.

"I think it may lead to nothing, but I certainly think it worth trying. If you cared to go, you would be the very person. Mrs. Erskine used to have a companion long ago, I'm told. She might like to have a bright and, if you'll permit me to say so, Miss, a pretty face about her."

Christine made her decision.

"I'm not going to pretend that it's what I wanted. And I don't think you'd be in the least deceived if I tried to hoodwink you. But I'll go, and if Mrs. Erskine asks me to stop with her I'll do it. I suppose I can always write to you?"

"I should want you to write a report every day and post it to my home address. I may not answer, but I shall get your letters all right, and if there is anything special I want, or that you can do, I shall let you know. You must arrange with some shop in Nice to keep your letters for you. Remember, Miss West, you mustn't forget that there may be enemies in the very household of Mrs. Erskine herself. I have no reason whatever to think so, but you must act as though there were."

"Do you know anything about her household?"

Pointer read her a letter he had received weeks ago in answer to one he had despatched to the Nice Prefecture. Mrs. Erskine lived a quiet but not secluded life in her charming villa, entertaining a little, and altogether enjoying the respectful esteem of the authorities. Her household was very simple. One man servant who was gardener and chauffeur, and one woman, his wife, who did the work, together with a first class cook. Mrs. Erskine only lived on one floor of her villa, the other two floors being let.

"I'm afraid I shan't be of any use," Christine said warningly; "it sounds quite out of my line."

The Chief Inspector would have preferred, as he had told her, to send a trained detective, but Christine was the only woman who would be able to enter under the aegis of a letter from Russell, and willing to work for the truth, so he encouraged her with the prospect of coming on some unconsidered piece of news which might set machinery in motion which would ultimately liberate Carter.

Finally she decided to go up to Perth personally and see the solicitor. Pointer looked up her train, and 'phoned about her to the Scotsman. Then, taking a hearty farewell of her, for the two liked each other, he went to the nearest 'phone and rang up for the second time that morning an American reporter friend of his on the London staff of the *New York Herald.*

"Pointer speaking. Have you looked her up? Good. Well, who did she marry? Beale, did you say? Mr. Beale? Oh, Mr. Edward Beale, only son of Mr. Augustus P. Beale, an editor of the *Universe.* I see. Eh? I only said I see. Thanks very much indeed;" and Pointer hung up the receiver and walked away, frowning deeply. So Miss Heilbronner, Robert Erskine's one time fiancee, had married Mr. Beale's only son. Did this stand for anything in the puzzle? If so, what?"

Christine meanwhile was speeding towards the rooms of Mr. Mortimer Meukes, the young solicitor to whom she had brought a letter of introduction from Canada yesterday afternoon.

"Did you see him?" she asked almost before she had shut the door behind her.

"I did, Miss West. He has agreed to retain me as his counsel, but I am bound to say that he refused to give me any information whatever." The young man gave a vexed laugh.

"Frankly, if I hadn't promised you to take the case, I should hand you back your retaining fee."

"I don't think you would." Christine spoke entreatingly. "You would be much too conscious of the fact that Mr. Carter is in a terrible position. He doesn't speak, obviously because there is some good reason why he can't, not because he won't."

"He doesn't even give that much explanation;" but Mr. Meukes' tone was less indignant.

"If you think Mr. Carter is a man to tamely or lightly submit to being broadcasted as a murderer and a thief, you can't have had a square look at him. Does he look a rabbit?"

Mr. Meukes hastily agreed that he certainly did not,

for Christine had spoken with warmth.

"Did he give you no message for me?"

"Yes, he told me to tell you, in strictest secrecy, that he was thankful you had come, and that if you could remain on this side of the Atlantic, as you told me to tell him you would, he might be very glad of your help later on. He was really most awfully touched by your coming and by your having sent me."

Christine told him that she was going abroad for some time possibly, unless Carter would prefer to have her stay closer at hand. She gave Mr. Russell's address to the solicitor and asked him to wire her Carter's reply.

Mr. Russell, like Pointer, took a liking to the Canadian girl. He sent off a letter at once to Mrs. Erskine recommending Miss West to her, and gave Christine a letter of introduction to hand her personally. "I'm sure she will welcome you. After all, the poor leddy has little enough that she knows about her only son."

Christine looked down her nose.

"I shouldn't build on that. Mrs. Erskine must be an iceberg."

Mr. Russell opened his eyes.

"My dear young leddy, anything but! Let me assure you she spends far too much on charity. Far too much."

"She let her 'only son' have a fearful struggle for years and years when she could have helped him, and never missed the money. She let the Mills for which he had worked so hard slip through his fingers at the last moment."

Mr. Russell was amazed.

"She sent him large sums of money regularly. I've seen his letters thanking her for the sums sent and asking for more and always getting it. Aye, always getting it. As for the last thousand pounds, he only asked for one thousand. I know what I am speaking of. The Chief Inspector could have told you the same."

Christine was bewildered. So bewildered that she held her tongue.

"Did you ever *see* the letters Robert Erskine wrote. I mean see them yourself?"

No, Christine had to acknowledge that she never had.

"Or any of Mrs. Erskine's letters to him?"

Christine had again to acknowledge that she never had seen one.

Mr. Russell nodded his head. "Just so. Just as I thought. Mrs. Erskine is a quiet, still woman. You might think her hard if you didn't know what lies behind her manner. My father could tell you of case after case of charity and goodness which he found out, after she had left Perth, of which she never spoke. She's not one to wear her heart on her sleeve, like all her family now dead and gone, but it's a heart of gold."

Christine bade Mr. Russell good-bye, and picked up a telegram from London in which Carter sent her word that any distance within a week's journey of London would serve him perfectly. She travelled up to town and on to Dover resolved to meet Robert's mother with a more unprejudiced mind.

It happened to be a singularly cold September, so that Mrs. Erskine had already returned from her Eze summer cottage to Nice, which presented a more animated appearance than usual, considering the month.

Villa des Fleurs was a beautiful house standing in a handsome palm garden where roses bloomed all the year, and Christine rang the bell of the first floor wondering what sort of experience lay before her. She was not often nervous, but she hardly noticed who was in the balcony to which the smiling French maid led her, until a white-haired woman, quietly but richly dressed, held out her hand.

Mrs. Erskine told her how pleased she was to see anyone who had known her husband and son in Canada, and asked Christine to stay at the villa for a fortnight.

"Though Nice is still quite deserted," she added.

Christine suggested that her wardrobe might not be quite up to Nice's standards, but Mrs. Erskine smiled faintly at the idea. She insisted on sending to the station where the luggage had been left, and Marie the maid showed the Canadian, after a delicious tea, into her room.

"We dine at eight o'clock," her hostess had told her. "The other people in the villa are friends of mine, and we have all our meals together. There is a Mr. and Mrs. Clark, who have the ground floor, and are splendid tennis players—you may like to practise with them of a morning—and then there is Major Vaughan, who has the floor above this. He is rather an original, but as an old bachelor, as well as an old friend of my husband's, I humour him."

The room assigned to Christine was very barely furnished. After a bath in a luxurious bathroom, she opened the door next to her own by mistake, and stepped into a really beautiful bedroom, all silver and petunia shades. Closing the door hastily, she raised her eyebrows a little as she stepped on into her own very comfortless nook. Mrs. Erskine might be delighted to see her, but, though she had had ample warning of her coming, she had certainly not been over concerned with her guest's comfort. At dinner, which was of a quality and served with a luxury Christine found a revelation, she met the other inmates of the house. Mr. and Mrs. Clark were a cheery, rather noisy couple, who seemed to consider all life a great joke. Christine decided that the lady had once been on the stage, from her partiality to paint and powder and richly tinted locks, but there was a breezy good nature about her which offset Mrs. Erskine's chilly manner. To Major Vaughan she took an instant aversion. His light eyes stared at her insolently, from the simple hair-dressing to the hem of her equally plain little frock.

"An almost-relation"—he repeated Mrs. Erskine's introduction; "you must adopt us, too, Miss West. We are all one happy family here, you see. Having everything in common." Christine thought she had never seen a more odious smile. She refused to talk to him, but all through the Clarks' chaff she could hear his biting speeches and neighing laugh. Mrs. Erskine's answers were chiefly monosyllabic, and before she joined the others at bridge under the palms and roses on the terrace she turned a rather weary face to the young woman.

"The Major is so brilliantly clever, when he cares to exert himself, that one has to overlook his little moods. After all, we shouldn't live like this if we didn't fit in very well together."

Which was more than Christine did. She sometimes thought it was her guilty conscience, the secret purpose which had brought her to Nice, that the villa seemed an uncomfortable place to her. Wherein lay the discomfort she could not analyse, even for Pointer's benefit. Mrs. Erskine took no interest in the open air life beloved by the Clarks, but lay for the most part on a chaise-lounge. The Canadian girl had heard of Scotch taciturnity, but her hostess was the most reserved person she had ever met. Only point-blank questions would bring out any of the remembrances on which Pointer had built his hopes.

Of her husband she spoke with a certain old-fashioned respect and affection that touched Christine. About Robert as a baby she spoke, too, and equally tenderly, but of his life after he left with his father for Canada, she either had nothing to say, or refused to say it.

"I would rather not discuss my son," she said once in her low, prim voice. "I am thankful that his murderer has been caught, but I dread what revelations the trial may bring to light."

Christine kept silence only by an effort. Rob had been no saint, but neither was his mother perfect. Shortly after her arrival her hostess had suggested that they should drive into Monte Carlo to make some purchases.

"There's a milliner I've heard of who's having a bankrupt sale of stock. I'm told there are really some good bargains to be got."

Christine and she drove down to where they were received by a very pale young woman, with dark shadows under her eyes, who looked as though a square meal would be a novelty. The hats were very moderately priced, indeed. Mrs. Erskine decided on a couple, and then began to dispute the price. Christine marvelled as she listened. It was a shabby scene, heightened by the air of triumph with which the Scotswoman turned to Christine when they were again in the car.

"They were bargains anyway, but I felt quite sure that I could get them still cheaper."

"She looked very sad, and so young," Christine said soberly.

"It takes capital to succeed in Monte Carlo," was Mrs. Erskine's rejoinder. Something in her companion's face arrested her attention, "You mustn't think me hard"— Christine did—"but I consider it wrong to spend a larger sum than necessary upon myself. Three-quarters of my income is needed for my charities, and the remaining quarter I consider I should stretch as far as possible."

Christine said nothing for a few minutes.

"It must be very nice to be able to give away so much," she said musingly, "but for that, I don't see that wealth has much to offer. Which is as well"—she turned to Mrs. Erskine with a smile—"as I am never likely to have much of it."

Judging by Mrs. Erskine's face, she did not share Christine's philosophical point of view in the least.

"A gipsy woman read my hand when I was a tiny tot and said that I should die a wealthy woman, and years later I had the same thing told me—that I should die possessed of great wealth."

They drove home in silence. Christine turned over in her mind what she had just learnt as to her hostess's division of her money. At first she was a little sceptical as to its literal truth, but after a week in the villa she took this suspicion back. Mrs. Erskine did live apparently on the scale of one thousand a year. Apart from the villa and its furnishings, which she had evidently purchased years ago, and the motor-car and meals which all the household shared, she spent but little on herself.

Of anything that could help John Carter Christine learnt nothing. Mrs. Erskine, though she had never heard of him before his arrest, now proclaimed his guilt as firmly as though he had already been tried and convicted. There was only one startling fact, after close on a fortnight, which the villa had revealed to Christine, and that was that Mrs. Erskine was afraid of something. She herself openly alluded to the fact, when discussing a case in the paper, that she slept with a loaded revolver under her pillow.

"Day or night I always have one close at hand, and I'm quite a fair shot."

"In the midst of life we are in death," cackled the Major, who had not shown himself for several days.

Mrs. Erskine looked at him with one of her frosty smiles, but said nothing. It suddenly struck Christine that here might be the reason why Mrs. Erskine kept the Clarks and the Major with her. They were even in the habit, she learnt, of sharing the summer cottage together, yet Christine did not think that Mrs. Erskine cared any more for them in her heart than she did for herself—Christine—whom yet she had asked to extend her visit for at least another fortnight.

Were they all not so much friends as a bodyguard? If so, from what danger were they intended to shield their hostess? She puzzled over the matter greatly. It seemed to her the one point of interest she had unearthed. As for Pointer, he wrote no comment, only that she was to watch every detail closely that came under her notice. True, she remembered Robert saying that his mother was timid, a timidity which he himself had inherited, just as he had her one uneven eyebrow, and also a little mannerism of the wrists which Christine never saw without remembering him with a pang.

Poor Rob, lying, after little but struggle and failure, in his family vault! If the living man and his danger meant more to her than the dead, not for that reason did she forget Robert Erskine's murder.

CHAPTER EIGHT

Christine had not accepted Mrs. Erskine's invitation to stay for another fortnight, but decided that another week at the villa would be the utmost she could afford to waste in futile efforts to learn some clue in a past to which no one referred. She was glad of her caution when one morning towards the close of her stay she found a letter for her at the shop where she had all her correspondence delivered. It was from Mr. Meukes. She tore it open with a beating heart, and read:

"Dear Miss West,

"I have had an interview with our friend. He was well, and sends you the following message which I have taken down word for word:—'Please be in Lille by September twenty-fourth. Do you remember my little contribution to your Toronto flat-warming party years ago? Go to that street. The number of the street you want is the age you were that birthday when we all got upset in the river. Go at midnight. Secrecy is vital, for the house may be watched. On the third floor ring the bell. Give no name, but ask for M. Meunier. He knows why I cannot come, and has instructions, left with him for just such an emergency when Rob died. In them I stated that in the event of my death you are my sole legatee, and that if I am incapacitated or prevented in any way from being present in the house at Lille on September 24th, you have full power to sign any documents for me. I enclosed your photo and a sample of your signature. He agreed to accept you as my proxy. For your further identification I wrote a password in the letter. It is the name we three gave our island at Four Winds, and he is to reply with the name of

*the rock on it. You can sign any papers M. Meunier hands
you without reading them; there will probably be only two.
M. Meunier will then give you a slip of paper on which he
will have written "Yes" or "No." Enclose this in a letter,
but send me (Meukes) a wire to say which word has been
handed you. If all goes as I hope, I may soon be able to
clear myself of at least one of the charges hanging over me.
If you are detained, wire Meunier at the address and sign
yourself "Minuit."'* There, Miss West, is the message he
sends you. He is still as obstinately silent on what
interests us as ever, but I do not wonder that you are fond
of him. He has a way with him. Will you allow me to wish
you good luck in your errand? I shall be glad to have a
wire from you to say that this is received and burned.*

    Very truly yours,
    Mortimer Meukes."

    Christine read the note very carefully. Entered a few
notes in her shopping diary under the heading of last
January, and as though they concerned dress items, and
burned the letter in the shop woman's stove before she
turned back towards the town itself and the villa.
    To-day was the eighteenth. Her visit would be up on
the twentieth. She decided to spend the days between its
end and the twenty-third at Avignon, among antiquities
which would well explain any lingering should eyes be on
her. She would have liked to go direct to Lille, but in a
town she did not know she doubted her ability to remain
unnoticed for so long. Of Mrs. Erskine and the inmates of
the villa she took a friendly farewell on the twentieth,
and caught the train to Avignon as she had mentioned in
conversation. Here she browsed among its Roman
remains and suffered its Roman wind till the twenty-
third, when she motored out to the next station on the
P.L.M. beyond Avignon and caught the Paris express, and
on to Lille. Arrived at Lille early in the forenoon, she took
a tram and saw the sights like any stranger. Only for
lunch did she allow herself to drift into the Rue des

Muguets. A café-restaurant almost opposite to No. 15 was her choice. She seated herself discreetly in an obscure corner, and had hardly finished a very good meal— Christine was no believer in a poached-egg day—when in walked Mr. Beale. She had his photograph inside her note-book at the moment. He paid no attention to her, but took a window-seat facing No. IS, and not only faced the large building but watched it intently. Once or twice he looked around, included her in his casual glance, and returned to his close watch. She laid down her paper.

"Isn't that M. Voiron?" She named a popular cinema actor as she paid her bill. Her tip made the waiter willing to linger.

"No, Madame," he obviously regretted to shatter an illusion, "that is un Anglais. He comes here lately daily and always to that table."

Christine seemed to be barely listening. That the house was also kept under observation by others for the rest of the twenty-four hours was obvious. She emptied her letter-case under the table into her hand-bag. It was a plain black leather case.

"I ask, because I saw him ahead of me in Rue Albert just now. He dropped this case. Will you please give it him at"—she glanced at the clock. It was exactly five minutes to two o'clock—"at two o'clock precisely. I do not want him to thank me personally, so please wait till two. "As it strikes!" The waiter assured her heartily, "Madame can count on me."

Christine saw that her watch and the clock were to the second together.

At exactly one minute past two she crossed the street and entered the door of No. 15, a door with many signs chiefly of insurance companies, and the men of the law in black and gold outside the handsome portals. She had noted how far into its open throat anyone on the opposite side could see. Just beyond this she flashed a glance backward. As she had hoped, Mr. Beale's head, with its fringe of reddish hair, was turned quite away from the window to the black-haired waiter standing beside him—her waiter.

She passed up the stairs in her silent galoshes. On the third floor was a sign: "Beauregard et Fils."

She looked at the landing from above. There was only one large door on each floor. No one was about. It was the sacred hour of noon repose.

She tried the top floor. This, too, belonged to a business firm, but a trap door on to the roof gave her her chance. It was a very dirty roof, but it had a high coping all round, and there was a place where she could sit down. She fastened down the trap-door, and made herself as comfortable as possible, with a novel she had with her, under her umbrella. At seven o'clock she lifted the flap gingerly and listened. Feet clattered down the stone stairs below her. Bang, bang! went the house doors far in the depths. The clerks were leaving. At eight o'clock she carefully crawled to the top landing and bent over the banisters. All was silent. She crept below. From the third floor came the sound of a typewriter. It was very dark inside the building, and she decided to remain on the fourth floor landing, at any rate for the present.

A little before nine o'clock she heard a key inserted in the hall door and steps ascending—cautious steps. They stopped at M. Beauregard's and out of the darkness came a gentle tap. Only one. Christine dared not risk a glance over the banisters. She was back against the wall above, listening intently. The door opened and shut swiftly.

She heard a man's voice say in English with a foreign accent: "The old idiot's working late, but he'll soon be gone. Everything is ready."

"The men understand their job, do they? Sure?" asked another voice with a distinct twang to it.

"If you come at twelve-thirty, monsieur, you will find that their job has been understood and perfectly carried out. Your birds will be trussed and waiting."

"You're still certain that you are not suspected?"

"Who, I? But no, monsieur, but no! A temporary clerk

who is open to reason will witness the signatures as well as myself. All goes well, *allez!*"

The men separated, one letting himself back into the flat and the other moving softly and slowly down the stairs.

Like a shadow Christine slipped after him. Near the house door she heard a click, and Mr. Beale switched on an electric torch for a second which gave her a glimpse of his face, before he swung open the door and shut it noiselessly behind him.

Another half-hour passed and she heard M. Beauregard's door again opened. This time it closed with a bang, and firm steps echoed down the stairs—no conspirator this apparently.

The minutes dragged by, till at exactly a quarter to twelve the front door was again unlocked, someone with an electric torch was coming up. A tall man, well muffled up, for the night was fresh. Christine slipped down to the door of the third floor flat, but keeping out of the ray of his steady light. The stranger come on, evidently making for the same goal. He got to the mat and extended his hands towards the little push button.

"*Ne sonnez pas, monsieur, ne sonnez pas!*" she murmured, touching his right arm.

"*Hein?*" He wheeled to face her, at the same moment the door was flung open and a clerk stood there bowing courteously.

"Come in, monsieur and madame. We did not expect a lady, but pray come in. I am M. Beauregard's head clerk."

M. Meunier entered briskly. For a second Christine hesitated. But what might be the effect of calling in the police? She stepped in, too. The door shut.

"This way"—and the clerk bowed them into a cheery office. "I go for the other witness."

Christine had exhausted her stock of French. She whispered hurriedly in English.

"M. Meunier, I am Christine West. There is something wrong. That man has confederates and a Mr. Beale is in it, too. After the signing—"

He gave her a reassuring glance.

"We, too, are prepared. The password, mademoiselle?"

"Suneverup. And yours?"

"Piratekeep."

The silly names from out her childhood seemed doubly incongruous just then, but as she looked him over, she guessed that M. Meunier would be a good man in a scrap. Tall, resolute, grey at the temples, and a bit red in the face, but with an eye like a boy's, and every short hair on his head bristling with vitality. Without a word he fastened his electric torch to the wall over by the door. She followed his example, hanging hers where he silently pointed beside a second door. She lit a candle which stood ready with matches and sealing wax on a desk in the middle of the room.

The head clerk entered, with a big stout German-looking man.

"M. Kaufmann, who will witness the signatures with me." The head clerk looked in surprise at the extra lights.

"It is said that there may be a strike of the electricians quite suddenly to-night," said M. Meunier shortly.

"*Tiens!*" muttered the head clerk, who did not seem to find the arrangements particularly welcome.

M. Meunier drew out two long papers from an inner pocket.

"We will sign now, mademoiselle, if you are ready. These are duplicates of one another. I shall keep the one, and the other will in due course reach our friend. I will sign first, and then if you will write your name here in this blank and then here"—he pointed out two blanks—"these gentleman will witness them both."

Christine watched his firm signature flourish. "Charles Bonnot"—the name of a member of the famous Lyons Silk house.

Then he handed her a pen and drew out a chair for her.

"Do not be nervous, mademoiselle," and his hand pressed her shoulder for a second to reinforce his meaning.

Christine felt her heart beating violently. It was all very well for him to reassure her, but they were but two against unknown odds.

She signed, and made way for the head clerk, who stood waiting for his turn, with one hand pressed on his waistcoat, and with a face now red, now white.

He, too, signed twice, and then moved away to the other side of the room. The burly M. Kaufmann bent over the table. Christine stared down at the first neat signature.

"You can go now, Kaufmann." The head clerk nodded to the door of an inner room on which his eyes had been riveted.

"Bon!" said the stout man obediently, "*bonsoir madame, bonsoir monsieur*." He held out his hand to the chief clerk, who snatched at it automatically.

There was a click, an oath from the head clerk, who stood twisting his wrists with handcuffs on them.

"Don't be alarmed, Miss West. It's me, Chief Inspector Pointer. I saw you read my name. M. Meunier and I thought we would let this gang hang themselves. As for the chaps he's shouting for, they're safely under lock and key in one of the cupboards, out of sight and sound. I can't have them taken away yet because of our friend, Mr. Beale. He's such a suspicious customer, and it's especially him I'm after." He turned to the clerk.

"Now look here." Pointer spoke excellent French —a war benefit. "If you want a lighter sentence assist the law now."

The man was utterly cowed. He burst into a flood of protests, excuses, and accusations of Beale, whose money had corrupted an honest man."

"Now look here," Pointer said again. "When Mr. Beale comes, open the door to him exactly as if nothing had happened. Close and bolt it behind him, and leave the rest to us. If you do this M. Meunier may put in a word for you to the police."

M. Meunier, who evidently believed in not interfering with another man's job, now nodded assent.

The clerk tremblingly assured them that he would do his very best.

M. Meunier again nodded. "It will be a question of twenty years for you if you do not," he threw in. The Chief Inspector went on to amplify his instructions.

"When Mr. Beale comes, show him in as I said. This room will be empty. I want him to talk before witnesses. Say that both messieurs—Mr. Beale need not know anything about this lady till afterwards— are tied up and are being guarded by the other men. Ask him for payment before you let him have the papers. Be sure and tell him explicitly that these are the papers taken by force from M. Meunier. You are a lawyer's clerk and understand what is wanted. We wish Mr. Beale to incriminate himself hopelessly before witnesses. We shall be listening with the door ajar. I shall open it wider when you are to hand the papers to the American. You understand?"

The frightened man said that he did and would do his best.

"It may make all the difference in your life how good your best is," M. Meunier warned him grimly.

Christine took an impulsive step forward.

"Oh, Mr. Pointer, what have you found out? Will it free John? Will it free him?"

"As to freeing him, that depends on himself, as you know, Miss West. If a man won't speak, won't give an alibi—"

"Ah, but he will now," put in M. Meunier; "the brave Carter! He can speak now. He signalled to me by means of the half-drawn curtain when he was arrested that he would say nothing till I gave the word. It was part of our contract, and vitally necessary, but the time for silence will have passed once these papers are in safe keeping, as they will be before morning. See, here is 'Yes'"—he handed her a slip of paper from his pocket-book—"that means just that to our friend—'Yes, you can speak. Yes, a great, an immense fortune is yours. Yes, all is well, and if we get M. Beale '"

"Hush!"

A light ring sounded at the door.

Pointer glanced at his watch.

"That's him. Now, then, Daru, see that you play your part well."

The man nodded eagerly. The three took their places inside the room which opened out of the one they had been in.

"But why aren't they in here? And the papers— the papers, where are they? Quick!"

"I have them," the head clerk answered calmly. He was acting most convincingly. "I have the papers, monsieur, but I think we should have a little further understanding before I hand them over. I think you should raise the price you promised if all went well. All has gone well. What do you suggest?"

Mr. Beale looked at him a moment in silence.

"Not one cent more will I pay. You don't know whom you're talking to. I'm not a man to browbeat. Our terms were generous and you accepted them. I don't say that we won't add an extra something if the papers are what we think, but that will be after they are in our hands, not before. And now, no nonsense, my man; I'm armed."

"Here are the papers, then," the clerk said sulkily.

Mr. Beale snatched them from him, then he spun around on his heel.

"Who signed—what—" his eyes had fallen on the signature of the second witness, "Alfred Pointer, Chief Inspector, New Scotland Yard, London."

"Evening, Mr. Beale." The signatory in person stepped into the room, bowed civilly, and passed on through the other door. "Come this way, Daru. M. Meunier wishes to talk with the gentleman."

Christine made a motion to follow, but the Frenchman

stopped her.

"By no means, mademoiselle. You represent the interests of your friend. Pray be seated here. Now, monsieur, let us have an understanding. These papers belong to me. Thank you"—as he took them over— "They are worth much to you?"

"It's a trap." Mr. Beale looked dangerous. "I see! It's a damned trap."

"But exactly! And behold you in it! In the very middle of it; and the trap, my friend, is a good one, very strong. Now, to begin again—on the one hand there is the 'phone there by mademoiselle, and the Prefecture, and a French prison—"

"I guess not! I'm an American, an editor of—"

The Frenchman shrugged amused shoulders.

"You may be an American, Monsieur, but I am a Frenchman, and this is France. I can assure you that we are no respector of persons here. You have broken French laws, and in a French prison you will assuredly stay for an unpleasantly long term unless you are shrewd enough to accept my terms."

"Well?" jerked out Mr. Beale.

"Mademoiselle, do you understand the position?"

"Not in the least."

"This man is a director in a very large silk spinning and weaving concern in America. Your fiance has made a marvellous discovery—an invention, epoch making, of an electric shuttle and a circular loom which permits of silk being turned out at about one-tenth of its present cost. When the first step of the idea came to him, he offered his patent to the Amalgamated Society. They did not understand its importance then, neither did he. They what you call 'turned it down.' He went on from that first step to other steps, and offered the patent to us. We could not believe it possible at first, but accepted it provisionally, provided it worked out as claimed. Meanwhile the Amalgamated had learnt something of the new discovery. Some tracing of a part must have fallen into their hands. They decided to kill it, for it is a revolution, this idea of Mr. Carter's. Mr. Carter met me secretly in Brussels and worked at a loom I built to his instructions. At first there were hitches, now here, now there, but at last has come absolute success. That was when Mr. Beale stepped in, and had him arrested for robbery. Diamond rings— pendants—bah! A huge fortune was already all but assured Mr. Carter. My firm could not finally sign, however, until a full trial at our own works had gone off successfully, and until we had had time to dispose of our existing stocks of silk. All this needed absolute secrecy. Mr. Beale, being in silk, knew this too. Part of the plans he may have, but the vital parts he could not be in possession of: Carter always kept those himself. Hence this night's planned robbery. He has had me watched, he has bribed my own secretary—so I have learnt from that clever police officer of yours, and now he thought the prize would be his; but, thanks again to Inspector Pointer, it is not so, but quite different. Now, Mr. Beale, here is my offer:—To forget this night's scene in return for a signed confession, given of your own free will, of course, that the jewels were being taken care of by Mr. Carter at your own request, which you had forgotten. That"—M. Meunier referred to his notebook—"M. Heilbronner withdraws his accusations and" —again he searched his notes—"and his warrant. That you both acknowledge that you have nothing against Mr. Carter in any way. Refuse this offer, and mademoiselle will ring up the Prefecture de Police."

Mr. Beale glared at his finger tips as though he would have liked to bite them.

"We have witnesses of the best," purred M. Meunier.

"I'll write it." Mr. Beale sat down at the desk, and rapidly filled a sheet of blue and white crossed paper which M. Meunier handed him. It was a clever piece of writing. Facts had just come to light, so wrote Mr. Beale, which entirely altered the case against Mr. Carter as far as the accusations of theft or embezzlement were concerned. The jewellery found in his trunk had been handed to him for disposal by a member of his (Beale's) family, unbeknown to that gentleman, and a careful examination of the books of the Toronto Mills showed that, though there had been errors in the book-keeping, there was none whatever in the percentages paid to the Amalgamated, which therefore gladly withdrew all claims against the managers, Robert Erskine, deceased, and John Carter, and were cancelling the warrants taken out mistakenly against them.

"Heilbronner'll sign it, of course, if I tell him to," Mr. Beale observed laconically. "One copy goes to our New York police, and one to Scotland Yard. Is that what you want?" Mr. Beale was certainly a good loser.

"*Parfaitment.*" The Frenchman opened the door and called in the Chief Inspector, who witnessed the American's signature, together with Daru.

Mr. Beale rose. "There, I'm through. I guess I'll go to my hotel."

"To mine, Monsieur, to mine, until Mr. Heilbronner signs these—you can post these to him to-night with a letter explaining your plight. Till then you stay with me, and M. the Chief, Inspector he stays, too, *hein?*"

"I'm on my holiday," assented Pointer equably, "and Lille is quite an interesting town. Go on ahead, Monsieur: Watts is below; he'll get a taxi for mademoiselle."

"Why didn't you stay and hear what M. Meunier had to tell about Jack, and the Amalgamated, and his wonderful discovery. To think he thought that he was no good at engineering!" Christine had asked Pointer to breakfast with her. She looked the ghost of herself after the excitements of the past night, but her eyes were alight.

"I didn't dare to go to sleep for fear it should be a dream."

"My dear Miss West, I haven't the faintest idea of what M. Meunier talked to you and Mr. Beale about," the

Chief Inspector said very seriously. "Mr. Beale's written retraction was given quite freely, an all-important point which we, none of us, must forget."

Christine digested this in silence.

"But how did you come to be there—how did you know about it all?"

"Routine," Pointer explained blandly; "routine took me to Geneva, where lived the avocat to whom Mr. Beale had once telegraphed, and where I found Mr. Heilbronner. From information which came to hand"—a vision of himself piecing together minute scraps from a dustbin made Pointer speak with unction—which came to hand, I found that Mr. Beale and he were extremely interested in a M. Meunier. I followed up this and that clue, and found that M. Meunier was M. Charles Bonnot of Lyons. More information coming to hand led to the belief that Mr. Beale, and incidentally Mr. Heilbronner, meditated getting hold of some important papers from M. Bonnot and yourself in Lille last night. M. Beauregard—one of M. Bonnot's men of business—took me on two days ago as an extra clerk for some special late work. Being an Alsatian explained my French, and no one suspected me."

"But—how did you know that *I* should be there?"

"I couldn't think of any better or firmer friend of Mr. Carter's." The Chief Inspector gave a little laugh, and Christine laughed too, and plied him with questions.

"What are you going to do when Mr. Heilbronner has signed? I suppose he will sign the papers?"

"I fancy he will. Mr. Beale is the strong man in that team." And Christine did not notice that he left the first part of her sentence unanswered.

"And what about that clerk?"

"Daru? Oh! M. Bonnot is letting him off very well. He will have to leave his present post, of course, but a place will be found for him at Lyons, where he can work up again. Mr. Beale offered what was a fortune to him, and he has a wife in hospital, so altogether M. Bonnot inclined to a very merciful view of things."

Christine herself waited in desperate anxiety. She could not go to England without knowing. The slip with "Yes" had been despatched to Carter, but she had been told to say nothing of the unexpected turn of events which Mr. Beale's detection had brought about.

The next day's post brought the papers signed by Mr. Heilbronner. Mr. Beale delivered the papers to M. Meunier with a wry smile.

"Satisfied now? Can I go to my hotel and leave this blank, blanked country?"

M. Meunier nodded, and Mr. Beale stalked from the room and drove off to his own suite in the Meurice. As he entered his sitting-room a figure rose from a chair. It was Pointer.

"Good afternoon, Mr. Beale."

"What does this mean? What the devil are you doing in my rooms?" There was no mistaking the fact that Mr. Beale's nerves were getting frayed.

"A few questions that we want cleared up," said Pointer imperturbably. "Shut the door, Watts. These papers, Mr. Beale, were found in your flat at Lyons."

"Well, suppose they were?"

"May I ask how they came into your possession, sir?"

"Bought 'em."

"From whom, sir?"

Mr. Beale's eyes travelled slowly from the papers to the officers and back from them to the papers.

"Off an agent of mine. His name would mean nothing to you."

"I must ask for it all the same, sir."

"Godard."

"I think not. Godard—Levinsky is his real name—told us, when we interviewed him at Lyons, that the papers in question were shown him by you, and that he made copies of them from which he worked."

Mr. Beale looked sallower than usual.

"I suppose it's got to be the truth. I took them out of Carter's bag."

"We have been in telegraphic communication with Carter about them. He says that these papers belonged to Robert Erskine."

"Quite possibly. But I got them out of Carter's bag just the same."

"Carter denies that absolutely. Mr. Beale, your situation seriously calls for frankness, as I'm sure you see for yourself. Things are very awkward. You have no satisfactory alibi for the hours from four to six on August fourth. Those screws which were found in Carter's box must have been put there by you. M. Meunier and two of his engineers give Mr. Carter an absolutely satisfactory alibi. They were with him all that Saturday afternoon and went down to Ostend in the train with him and saw him off on the boat. Those screws, these papers of Erskine's, and his note-book, look very ugly, taking into consideration the reason your firm had for getting Carter and Erskine out of the way, and the fact that you and the manager, together or separately, were in No. 14 for a considerable time on that Saturday afternoon."

Mr. Beale's sallowness became tinged with green.

"It's like a Sunday-school story," he said after a pause, "illustrating the way of the transgressor. I guess I know when the ice won't bear me. Chief, those papers and that note-book are Erskine's. You're right there. But I didn't get them off his dead body, nor yet kill him, either before or after. I bought them from the manager. Yes, sir, from the manager, and for one thousand five hundred pounds in notes. I had the sum on me, for I hoped to meet Carter and do a deal with him. Now, as to the motive—you're talking nonsense and you must know it. Carter was our man. Erskine staked him, but Erskine's death wouldn't have helped us any. It did quite the other way. We didn't want all that limelight turned on us, I do assure you. As to the screws— well-1, possibly I did let them drop into Carter's box by mistake. We wanted him fixed up a bit, as he wouldn't deal. Mind you, he only had to speak out to've left his prison the next day. If he chose to stay there that wasn't my fault. I guess he was afraid to speak, for if you *really* think Carter had no hand in Erskine's death— well, your brains aren't what I assess them at. As to my alibi . . . I spent the time exactly as I told you. Trying to locate Carter, who was in one of the Southampton Street hotels. I gave up trying to find his name, guessed that he was using another, and, acting on a belief of my man's that he had seen him go into the Enterprise, tried there. I took room number fourteen without an idea as to whose it really was, and the rest happened exactly as I told you, except that I lifted the top off the wardrobe after what I had seen through that knot-hole, but I couldn't see Erskine's face because it was turned sideways and downwards, as you remember. Also my torch had given out. Had I guessed whose corpse was in—but there . . . The match I lit I took from those vestas on the mantelpiece, and I dropped one into the wardrobe. I saw you salvage it, Chief."

"Did you wash your hands in the basin?"

"Sure, and threw the water on to the balcony. It looked as though I had washed my boots in it. The top of that wardrobe would have made a first rate flowerbed. Well, to continue my tale of sin, curiosity made me have a look among the dead man's effects. I carry a pass key because of that damned Carter. I saw nothing interesting, and went for the manager, whom I found prowling about outside in the corridor. He seemed fairly knocked off his perch, but I sometimes wonder— However, he certainly would have had to have a nerve to put me into a room with a murdered man, if he knew anything about it. Yet—well, I don't quite know what to think; he and Carter may have had an understanding of some sort."

"Humph!" There was a long silence. "You hadn't been to the hotel earlier in the day, then?"

"No."

"Did you step out on to the balcony at all?"

"Not once, but I thought I heard someone moving outside the window while the manager and I were talking, just before you arrived, and I pulled up the blind. As I did so I think a window clicked shut beside me."

"Beside you? Which side?"

"The Enterprise side. It sounded like the next room, but I couldn't swear to that."

"Humph! How did you come to buy those papers from the manager?"

Mr. Beale thought a while.

"He offered them to me. I said that though I didn't know Eames personally yet I knew that he was mixed up in a business swindle. Said I'd be mighty glad, had I known who he was, to've had a look through his papers. He sat still a moment, then went out and came back with that pocket-book and those papers you have there, done up in a neat little green and white packet. Didn't say how he got them, and I didn't ask. No, sir, I didn't ask!"

"Humph! Well, Mr. Beale, you've only yourself to thank for your position. I shall leave two of my men to accompany you till we look into matters a little more, and you'll have to stay in England."

"Under arrest, am I?"

"Not at all, sir. Under close supervision—at present. Of course, if you were to try to escape . . ." The Chief Inspector left the consequences to Mr. Beale's alert imagination; "but you'll find Watts here and Duncan know their work, and will cause you as little inconvenience as possible."

"I see. Well, I know when a game's lost," the American retorted bitterly. "Say, you spoke of Carter's alibi just now. I suppose he's free, and all that?"

"He will be by to-morrow"; and Pointer, after reading over Mr. Beale's account and getting it signed, made off for the nearest telegraph office, while the American looked after him with an ironical smile. "Carter to be set free to-morrow. Well, well, the brains of the British police!"

Christine was the first to arrive in London, where she was met by a pale, gaunt-faced young man. Pointer, carrying the signed paper which Mr. Beale had staked so much to obtain, followed, and with him, though in a different compartment, travelled Mr. Beale and his valet.

The Chief Inspector, after an interview with the authorities at the Yard, went on to the Enterprise Hotel. The manager was in, and he practically repeated his opening words to Mr. Beale.

The manager might or might not be made of better stuff than the American, but he certainly was of softer. He sank back into his chair, looking as though he saw the hangman already entering his cell.

CHAPTER NINE

The Chief Inspector gave the manager no time to collect himself. He went rapidly over Mr. Beale's accusation that it was Mr. Hughes who had offered the papers of the dead man to him.

"I'm in an awful hole." The manager poured out a glass of whisky and soda with a shaking hand.

"Pretty bad," agreed the unsympathetic police-officer, "but perhaps it might be worse." His glance around the room pointed his meaning. The tumbler was set unsteadily back on the tray.

"I'm a ruined man in any case. I might as well have thrown up the sponge when you came last time—"

"Perhaps," murmured Pointer.

"—but here's the true story. You can take it down, and I'll sign it here before we go to the police-station, or you can arrest me first and have it afterwards."

"Let's have it here."

"Well, the case was exactly as I told you up to that moment when Beale and I sat here after you had gone, talking over the suicide. I jumped up, for I suddenly remembered after all that Eames—I mean Erskine—*had* given me a cardboard box to keep in the safe. I had joked him about it, saying it looked like a box of chocolates, and he had said it wasn't much more important, but still he wished me to take care of it for him. Without thinking—for it is one of my strictest rules that I never go to the safe without the booking-clerk or the hall porter with me, and never in the presence of a visitor, I unlocked the combination and opened it. That shows how rattled I was by what had just happened. I pulled out the box—"

"Wrapped in green and white striped paper?"

"That's the one. And I said something about 'Good God, I forgot to speak of this to the police.' I moved towards the door when Mr. Beale stopped me. He was tremendously excited, and said that as soon as he had seen Eames' face in the full light he had recognised him as a dangerous crook whose partner, and doubtless murderer, he (Beale) was after. In fact, he stuffed me with the same yarn he filled you up with when you arrested Carter."

The Chief Inspector gave no sign that he felt the dig.

"He declared that the box would contain plans and signals in cipher for the use of the gang. Would I let him have a look at it? I finally—well, I refused at *first*"—the bitterness of the manager's voice told the whole story—"but you know what a way Mr. Beale has with him. He claimed to recognise the plan of his own house in the note-book, and then—I'd just been letting myself go a bit about what a blow the suicide would be to the hotel, which was having its work cut out to keep its head above water—he referred to that. Said that he wanted a scoop for his paper. Finally he offered me one thousand pounds down on the table for the box, and I let him take it for another five hundred. Mind you, I'm not trying to clear myself, but I believed his story. And of course when you arrested Carter I thought what a Quixotic fool I should have been to have acted differently."

He stopped and had another drink.

"But that isn't all that you have to tell."

"You mean the pages torn out of the receipt-book. You know about them."

"No, I don't mean them. I know all about that, as you say. I mean something else."

"Do you want my confession as to how I killed Eames?" asked the manager sardonically.

"I want to know first who the man was you showed over the balcony rooms, including No. 14, at midday on Saturday, August third?"

"That was Sikes. He lends money strictly on the q.t.

and at only seven hundred per cent. But the mere idea that his little hobby might get about infuriated him so that after you sent that blundering chap of yours down to investigate he broke the whole thing off. He's aiming to get into Parliament: that's why he's Sykes with a 'y' now."

"Humph! And had you never seen Erskine before?"

"Never."

"Nor Mr. Beale?"

"No. I assure you, Inspector, that I had never seen either man before."

"And now about those 'phones on Saturday at five o'clock?"

But the manager could only repeat that he knew nothing more than he had already told the police. He could not recollect 'phoning at all about five o'clock; but if he had, it had been a vain attempt to get through to his hatter."

The police-officer asked him to sign his statement.

"We *may* not have to use it—"

The manager drew a deep breath.

"—but, of course, you must keep yourself within touch of our people. And now, Mr. Manager, what can you tell me about what has become of the occupants of rooms eleven and twelve?"

The manager looked over his papers.

"Mrs. Willett left an address in Devonshire to which her letters were to be forwarded. The hall-porter has it, I suppose."

"Yes, but Mrs. Willett did not go there. The Devonshire hotel has no knowledge of her whereabouts beyond the fact that she wrote from here, and engaged a room on August 16th."

The manager was unable to help.

"Now as to Miss Leslie, the occupant of number twelve. She left here on September seventeenth, and all inquiries at the theatre only show that no one has her address. Apparently she has gone away in the midst of an engagement without leaving a trace of her plans."

Here, too, the manager was not able to offer any help.

Pointer swung himself on his homeward bus, not overpleased with his men. He had given orders that the occupants of the balcony rooms were to be kept under constant surveillance, and the two most important ones had slipped away into the unknown. Miss Leslie he had tried to trace through the Thompsons, father and son, and even through the Blacks, but all to no purpose.

"Mrs. Able has very tactfully chosen roast veal," O'Connor jibed as he took his seat at the table. "Now, wanderer, what of thy goings to and fro?"

Pointer merely raised his eyebrows and asked what was under the other cover, and not until the meal was well out of the way and he had lit a pipe did he give a rapid review of his "holiday tramp."

O'Connor thought that the green and white scrap of paper backed up the manager's rather than Beale's version of the selling of the papers, and Pointer agreed that it might, but he did not say how much of the rest of the tale of either man seemed to him likely.

Next morning he had a long interview with Carter, and found that, as he thought, the Canadian had arrived on July twentieth in London. He had expected to go straight to a hotel as near Erskine's as possible, but on arrival at Liverpool Street Station he had been handed a telegram from "Meunier," instructing him to come on to Brussels at once. Erskine had come to meet the train, after engaging a room for him at the Marvel and one at the Enterprise for himself. The connecting balcony was too good to lose, so at their hurried meeting in a corner of the refreshment room, where they posed as strangers, one of whom handed a newspaper to the other and discussed the weather for a moment, it was arranged that Erskine was to write to the Marvel in Carter's name, enclosing enough money to retain number two, while Carter rushed off to Dover and Ostend. Ten days later Carter had to come back to London to buy some special tools he could not get in Brussels, and had spent a couple of hours with

Erskine. It was on his way to the night boat-train that he had bought him the cough medicine. When he had returned again on the fatal Saturday night of August 3rd it had been for the express purpose of telling his "pard" that success was certain. The sight of the policeman when the window opened warned him that something was wrong. After an interval he had crept out on to the balcony again and peered into the room. He could see only an empty bed and Miller on guard. Full of anxiety, he had to start back for Brussels at once, followed, though he did not know it, by Beale. Then came hours of torturing uncertainty, and finally the few lines in an English paper telling of "Eames' suicide." Carter could hardly bear to speak of it. But they had each bound themselves before starting from Canada that in case of danger they would separate at once, and in case of any accident to the one, the other would "carry on"; also he was under the most solemn pledges of absolute secrecy to M. Bonnot. So in bitterness of soul he worked on, only determined to avenge his friend's death some day.

"And that day's now, Inspector. I won't rest till I find out who it was that killed Rob, though, mind you, I don't have any doubt as to the man's identity. But I'll work night and day to get the proof."

"You think it's—"

"Beale. Of course. So do you, I guess. He didn't know how few papers Rob had on him. Just because I thought it was dangerous, I didn't give Rob anything of real importance, and those few I did let him have were only because he insisted on our sharing the risks together. Of course, Beale murdered him after he found Rob wouldn't do a deal, which I don't doubt he tried first. Then he did his best to get me out of the way, because he knows well enough that I won't find life worth living till the man who did it is hung. When I came home that night in Brussels earlier than usual from my work and found Beale at my desk I wish to heaven I had killed him instead of merely trussing him up and beating it to Lille. But my pledge to

Bonnot tied my hands. They're free now." Carter stretched them out along the table. Long, lean, nervous hands. "At Lille, the little ferret fastened on me again and pretty nearly did for me."

"Pretty nearly," agreed Pointer.

"It was a facer," Carter repeated sombrely. "You see, I didn't know whether I had an alibi for Rob's murder or not, for I didn't know what hours were the vital ones, and I had been back in London, I had been on the balcony, I remembered even the couple of boxes of vestas I'd left Rob, and wondered if they would help to trace me out. And suppose I got clear of the charge of having murdered my pard, I was done for by the American frame-up. Only your catching Beale, and the way M. Bonnot handled him, saved me. They wouldn't have let me off under twenty years over there. Beale has tremendous political influence through his paper. The police officer who put the warrant through was some sort of a hyphenated Yank out for a political job."

"Just so. Yes, I see." Pointer turned to his notebook. "Now, to go back to Erskine. Can you tell me what was the cause of the split between him and the Heilbronners?"

"Rob never told me in so many words. He was in love with Mattie Heilbronner, you know—Christine told me she'd given you the points of the case as far as she knew them—but it was some trouble at the factory at the beginning of the war that started it all. He believed that he had stumbled on some devilish German plot to poison the bandages. The mills were turning out hospital supplies, you know. He was certain that old Heilbronner was at the back of it, and after that all was over between them but the burial. Yet even so, when I had knocked my first idea into workable shape, he insisted that the fair thing to do was to offer it to the Amalgamated. They turned it down and began hounding Rob and me out of the business. I won't go into it all, but it only stiffened us. I worked my ideas into something better and tried Bonnot of Lyons. It was really while I was lying in the hospital

there that I had come across a replica of an old loom
which gave me my first glimmering of an idea. Bonnot
told you himself how he took the thing up—cautiously at
first and then enthusiastically. The difficulty, however,
for Rob and me was to get to Europe. We decided to use
Mrs. Erskine's money for that purpose, as it wouldn't
save the mills, and started away by different boats under
assumed names. And now, Inspector, will you let me help
you? Or must I try on my own, or with a private detective,
to solve the how and the why of Rob's death? *Who* did it I
feel pretty sure of, as I said."

Pointer decided quickly. He could easier keep Carter
under observation in France than in England. To have
had a hand in his partner's death, that death that
removed from him the necessity to repay past loans, that
left him in undisputed possession of a huge fortune,—he
must have had an accomplice. Any effort to communicate
with the actual poisoner would be far more difficult to
carry out undetected in Nice than in London.

"Thank you, Mr. Carter, for your offer. I am starting
as soon as I can get away for France—for Nice. I shall be
very glad if you care to come—"

"Care to come! You bet I do!"

"But you understand that it may be some time before
I can ask your help. There is a good deal of clearing up
work—mere routine—to be done first." His tone implied
that when a stroke of real genius was felt to be needed,
Carter's hour would come.

"I quite understand. As long as I can hope to be of any
help—at any time—I'll come. Christine feels as I do. We
can't marry until this thing is cleared up. She's as keen
on seeing justice done Rob as I am, or nearly so. He
wasn't her partner as he was mine. If you'll come
downstairs we'll go around to her hotel and hear what she
says for herself."

Christine had treated herself to comfortable rooms in
a quiet hotel near Baker Street. She was as emphatic as
Carter that the one thing for them to do now was to find

out and bring to justice the murderer of Robert Erskine. "Though I certainly wasn't much of a help to you?" Her voice made it a question.

"Oh, I don't know about that. I don't deny that I hoped you might have got hold of some direct clue while at the villa,—but that's always a matter of luck, and Mrs. Erskine looks the kind of woman to keep her own confidence—or the confidence of another, even supposing she knows more than she chooses to say. Besides, remember you gave the very important tip of the loaded revolver which she keeps at hand, and the suggestion about her body-guard, as you think her friends may be."

"You don't agree with me?"

The police-officer laughed. "Pointer's away on his holiday. Impenetrable official reserve is the order of the day now, and on your and Mr. Carter's part absolute, unquestioning obedience. Is that a bargain? Thank you; I was sure that you would both see the necessity for my making that an essential of your co-operation. And you must be patient, Miss West. As I told Mr. Carter, there'll be a lot of spade work to be done, if we are to discover any clues at Nice, before there can be any question of either of you helping."

Like her fiance, Christine said she did not care how long she had to wait, if only she could be of some use.

"Very well, then, we quite understand one another." Pointer seemed regardless of the fact that Carter's real thoughts were a subject of much doubt to him, and that some of his speculations about them were very far from being understood by that young man—"and agree that no plan can be drawn up until I have reconnoitred thoroughly."

"Would it be a help," asked Christine, "if I were to stop with Mrs. Erskine again?"

"I can't say yet."

"I don't think I like the Chief Inspector as much as I did Mr. Pointer." Christine's smile robbed the speech of its bluntness.

"Oh, don't say that!" implored the officer. "Do be original and have a good word for the police! But now about our going. Mr. Carter can start at once. I shall follow by the day after to-morrow at the outside. If you"— he turned to the Canadian—"will put up at, say, the Negresco or the Angleterre, I shall find your name at once and be able to get into touch with you. Should we meet by chance, we are, of course, strangers. And you, Miss West, if you will let Mr. Carter know where you are stopping near Nice"

"It won't be Avignon!"

"—you could meet quietly. But not more than once a week, please, and, naturally, always at different places and on different days. Through him I shall have your address, and if you'll excuse my addressing you inside any letter or telegram or 'phone as Miss"—his eyes fell on an open magazine—"Miss Gladys—"

Christine shivered.

"—you will know that the message is from me. What name are you going by, Mr. Carter?"

"Crane."

"Good, and you are starting?"

"To-night, if I can get a ticket. But for God's sake don't let Beale slip through your fingers. Mark my words, *he's* the man!"

"He won't slip." Pointer shook hands and walked briskly away. He had arranged matters to his liking and his plans were in his own keeping. He wired to the Nice police to be ready to keep an observant eye on Mr. Crane. He would have been glad of the Canadian's immediate help, but he intended to take no risks of confusing the trail.

Pointer's first act on arriving at Nice was to 'phone up the Canadian at the Negresco. Over the wire he obtained a minute account of the way he had spent his two days on the Cote d'Azur. Then he rang up his police friend, and Carter's account of himself was verified in every particular. So far so good. He next presented himself at

Mrs. Erskine's. That lady was lying down with a severe headache when his card was taken in to her, but she sent him out word to please call back later, as she very much appreciated his having come to see her. Pointer found her quite full of questions—for her—as to Carter's release. She evidently feared that the police had been hoodwinked by some plausible villain.

"I'm not a revengeful woman," she explained with her plaintive Scotch accent, "but I do not want the murderer of my son to escape."

The Chief Inspector had apparently no explanation to offer beyond the fact of Carter's belated, but absolutely water-tight, alibi.

"Well, of course you must know your business best," she murmured from among her cushions, "but it would take more than a Frenchman's word to have made me set that man free!"

She asked very kindly after Christine, and he did not mention the fact of that young lady's coming marriage to the object of Mrs. Erskine's suspicions.

Mrs. Erskine evidently feared that it would be quite useless, but she had not the slightest objection to his going over again all the Erskine letters in her possession.

"But Robert's letters are missing. You remember the packet I showed you in Paris?"

Pointer did.

"When we returned here—Mrs. Clark came to fetch me: she thought I was too ill to be left to Marie's care alone—the letters had gone. I am sure I placed them in the top of my trunk, or saw Marie put them there just before we started. I had them under my pillow before that. But when Marie unpacked here there was no sign of them. On the whole, I am not sure that their presence was not more of a grief than their absence. But I confess the thought of those letters, sacred to me by my loss, having been lost by some carelessness—" She paused with a worried frown.

It was nearly half past eleven before Pointer made his

appearance on the following morning.

Mrs. Erskine had had an old trunk brought down from the attic in which, as she sent him word, she kept everything belonging to family matters of any kind.

There were several letters from Mr. Henry Erskine which were new to the officer. They were all affectionate in tone. It was quite clear from them that he only contemplated remaining away a twelvemonth on his brother's ranch. In all of them, however, there was no faintest clue, no hint of any mystery. The rest of the box concerned the Abercrombies more than the Erskines, and the Chief Inspector gained a very good idea of the stiff but honourable upbringing of Margaret Erskine from them. He went through them and the old books, old bills, and personal trifles which the trunk contained with amazing speed and thoroughness. Then he shut the lid and stood awhile in thought. As he stood there, he heard a soft thud in the next room. To a practised ear, there is only one thing which makes that sound. A safe-door was being closed in the wall adjoining. A few minutes later he heard Mrs. Erskine speaking from the room beside him. She told Marie to be on hand to let out the gentleman—she had referred to the Chief Inspector as connected with her firm of lawyers—as soon as he should be finished. She did not mention refreshments, he noted, though the day was hot, and the work dry and dusty. Like Christine, Pointer saw that the good lady did not encourage unnecessary expenditure.

He heard her deliberate steps cross the marble hall and the front door shut. He heard Marie go into her mistress's room. Like a shadow he stepped into the drawing-room, of which the door stood open. From an oriel window he looked down at the car waiting below. There was a man sitting in one of the front chairs and a handsome, painted, plump woman on the back seat, dressed in the very height of fashion. Pointer eyed her keenly through his glass from a discreet position behind the curtains. Her black eyes were fastened on the front door. These were evidently the Clarks, and even after Mrs. Erskine had taken her seat he kept his glass levelled until the car turned up the drive and purred out of sight.

He slipped back into the little room where the trunk still stood, and when the maid looked in, after tidying the bedroom next door, she found him apparently hard at work. He glanced up cheerily, to meet a very gloomy stare.

"It's going to be a long job, eh, monsieur?"

"Looks like it. By the way, I forgot to say something to madame. At what hour does she return?"

"Only just in time to dress for dinner. There is a great charity bazaar on at the Castle at which madame has promised to help. She gave us all tickets for the grounds."

"Were you going, too? I heard that there were to be all sorts of amusements."

"I was going, but, if you wish it, I can stay . . .?"

Hope shone in her face again. Perhaps the jaunt would yet come off.

"No! no!" protested Pointer in genuine horror. "I may be here for hours."

A bank note was slipped into her hand. "Go and enjoy yourself, *ma fille*, and drink my health at lunch."

Marie was in the seventh heaven, what with the chance to get off for the day after all, the twenty francs, and the compliment to her thirty years. Within a quarter of an hour a voiture, with Marie, her husband, the chef and Mrs. Clark's maid, drove off briskly; for, as Marie said, in what better hands could the villa be left than in that of a gentleman connected with madame's solicitors?

Pointer bolted the doors, and then walked rapidly through the house from cellar to attic. Major Vaughan and his man were away at Monte Carlo, the maid had told him, and he had it all to himself. He took his coat off, and after his rapid general survey examined the rooms in detail. Finally he came to Mrs. Erskine's bedroom. The walls were of grey silk, with here and there grey velvet medallions. After a little measuring he made for the panel beside the window. As on all the others, oxydised metal traceries ornamented the oval. He pressed an ornament which looked the shiniest to his keen eyes. A very few experiments taught him the trick, and the panel swung open on its hinges. At the same time three gongs clanged in muffled fury. Pointer had spent some of his minutes, as he went over the house, to good effect in stuffing sofa cushions around all electric alarums, or the din would have been terrible. The telephone bell beside the bed rang insistently.

"'Ello! 'Ello!" he called in answer; "yes, it is I, Guillaume, and not a burglar. It was as well I had that little chat with you this morning, eh?" and he hung up the receiver. Then he turned back to the safe. A few minutes went by before even his skilled eyes found the right knob which should have been turned first to silence the alarums. The safe had been bought off a firm which had spared no expense in its installation evidently. It was the only one on the premises, and he hoped to find some interesting things in it. He looked at the safe sitting like a shrine deep in its little niche with great respect. "So it's an Aglae. Humph!"

The Aglae safes, turned out very sparingly by Creusot, are the last word in their line. He knew them well. There was one in the Commissioner's office at the Yard. They are pretty to look at. No cumbersome, easily detected combination lock here. A little slit, looking as innocent as a slot-machine, faced him, but any key, whether of another Aglae or not, which was not the right one would set a powerful alarum ringing against the light metal of the outer door which no cushion could deaden, and it would ring until the right key was inserted, if need be for thirty-five days. If a burglar, caring nothing for keys, tried his usual tactics of cutting, he would find an outer case which let itself be opened with ease, and out would stream a volume of gas calculated to render anyone unconscious who stood near it, even though the windows

were open. Some Aglae had an alternative plan by which
a revolver emptied its six cartridges in the direction
where the first cut was made. Altogether, a slight
acquaintance with an Aglae was distinctly advisable for
any up-to-date cracksman if he wanted a chance to show
his talents elsewhere.

Pointer whistled softly. There was only one man in
Europe who could help him. In Barcelona, at the foot of
Tibidabo, lives a Catalan, a Senor Foch, who works in a
simple little shop with his son for the police of seven
countries; and lucky it was for the police that honesty had
been the motto of the two men, for there is nothing that
can be done to lock or key that they cannot do. Only a
Foch could copy the key of this safe, supposing Pointer
could lay his hands on it for a moment. The Catalans
worked only on their own terms. Measurements, weight,
and impressions had to be taken, according to their strict
rules, or they would refuse the job.

He replaced everything as he had found it, took off the
silencers from the various alarums, and proceeded with
his room to room inspection. In Major Vaughan's flat he
found some things which interested him greatly. He even
went so far as to take a tracing of some boots and shoes
he found up there, and very familiar the outline would
have looked to Watts, too, had he seen it.

It was close on six o'clock when he finished, and the
only results to the eye for a very fatiguing day was a little
cardboard box of a kind which had contained stationery, a
tiny oval box retrieved from a dusty corner of the attic,
and a little yellow pill-box, marked "Mrs. Erskine, 14
Ave. de Paris, Biarritz," that had come from a deep pocket
of an old travelling bag. Yet with these, and his tracings,
and his other discoveries, the Chief Inspector felt more
than satisfied.

Next morning he took his leave of Mrs. Erskine, and
acknowledged that she had been right in thinking that
the papers which he had looked over contained no clue.

"I'm quite sure that the criminal is that man you let

go, Carter!"

He did not contradict her. "He's where we can put our hands on him at any moment," he assured her as he bowed himself out. He had timed his departure to concide with the hour at which he had learned from Marie that the major and his man were expected to arrive from Monte Carlo. The major would sometimes go regularly to the Casino for a week at a time, or, as now, just for an occasional flutter; on the other hand, months might go by without his trying his luck at the tables, where he generally won. And indeed a week might pass without his leaving his flat at all. He had been gassed in the war, Marie informed Pointer, prompted by his easy questions, "and was now *un original—un sauvage*, yet often still of a charm!"

The major returned in a dusty motor while Pointer still lingered over some flowers behind a bush of heliotrope. The valet whipped open the door. The major, a shrunken little man, stood blinking irritably into the sunlight with red-rimmed eyes. He caught sight of the Clarks just leaving in their tennis clothes.

"You look like solid ghosts," he grunted in reply to their greetings.

"Won pots of money, you lucky man?" asked the lady.

"Oh, pots and pans!" he nodded. "As you say, I am a lucky devil. Know the difference between a lucky devil and an unlucky one, Clark. You *ought*, by Gad, but *do* you?"

Mr. Clark, a sunburnt, good-natured looking man, apparently gave it up.

"A lucky devil helps to skin others, an unlucky one can only be skinned," and the major, with the cackle Christine so much disliked, walked into the house.

"Of a charm certainly! repeated Pointer to himself with a faint grin as he emerged from behind the flowering shrub and walked down to the police, where his snapshot of the major was developed and enlarged, in time for a copy to be despatched to the Yard in the evening, together with a pressing request for further particulars as to the officer in question.

Carter was next met in Pointer's quiet room at a Meuble near the station. The detective officer had no directions to give the Canadian, but asked a good many questions about Robert's letters, and to the answers he paid the closest attention. That done, he took his departure by the afternoon express. He got out at Marseilles, where he waited for Watts to join him. That detective had been instructed by telegram to leave Mr. Beale to the sole care of his mate and join the Chief Inspector at the noisy, dirty port as soon as possible. Watts was only too glad to descend from the crowded train and make his way to the hotel, where Pointer gave him an account of the past day's work.

"I don't want amateur help!" Pointer examined some *bouillabaisse* with quite undeserved suspicion. "Carter, even supposing he were free from suspicion—which he isn't—may be a useful chap, or may be an absolute bungler. I haven't time to train budding talent in this case."

"And the young lady?"

"Is staying at Cannes. She's very keen to help, and I don't say that she may not be useful, too; but give me the real thing, Watts. Had I been able to get a good woman-detective into the villa in her place, a good many doubts as to the character of Mrs. Erskine's 'body-guard' might be over. However, I couldn't."

Two nights later a loud ringing and banging on the door of the villa disturbed the occupants just after they had separated for the night. It was quite late, for they had all been to a theatre and supper party. A postman stood at the door. Could he see Madame Erskine about a cable which had come, marked "Urgent," and which he was not sure was meant for her, as beyond the name there was no address.

Mrs. Erskine, whose bedroom lights had only been twinkling a short time, put her head over the windowsill and said that she would come down at once. The man was told to enter, and the front door closed.

A figure crouching behind some bushes sprang lightly erect, waited a moment or two, listening intently at a shuttered window—the window into the lower hall—then, lifting a ladder lying buried in the earth, stood it deftly against Mrs. Erskine's window ledge, and was up with the swiftness of a cat. He took off his rubber shoes and left them on the sill. Then he swung himself into the room and looked at the safe. The door stood wide open, the key was in it. In a second the black figure slipped to the bedroom door. Mrs. Erskine had left it locked. He strode back to the safe, took out its key and weighed it carefully, though swiftly, on a little balance. Followed several quick measurements taken with a sort of dialled spanner, after which four impressions had to be made in boxes containing the special Foch compound. Balance, spanner, and boxes were returned to a little black bag the man wore strapped to his waist. This done with the utmost but unflurried haste, the key was replaced in the safe, and the figure vanished the way it had come. The ladder was laid on the grass for a moment, till the ground under the window had been smoothed with a rake-head, also produced from the bag. In another minute ladder and man seemed to melt, rather than to pass, through the gate.

The telegram was not for Mrs. Erskine after all, as a glance at its obviously business contents told her. It took some time to make this clear to the postman, who was an "extra," and spoke with an atrocious Basque accent—acquired during the retreat from Mons, when Watts' company had got inextricably entangled with some of the blue Berets. Finally the postman grasped the truth, apolgised, and "returned to the post office to make further inquiries." These seemed to lead him to a small hotel in a back street, after a change of toilet in the nearest dark doorway, which included turning his coat inside out, ripping off some narrow red braid from each trouser leg, and substituting one cap for another. That done, Watts went to bed, to speculate with some curiosity on exactly what had taken place in the villa during the colloquy in the central hall. He knew better than to ask his superior, and finally consoled himself with the thought that he would doubtless hear of it some day under "From information which has just come to hand."

CHAPTER TEN

Eight o'clock next morning found the Chief Inspector wrapped in slumber. The Boots interrupted them to tell him that there was an insistent telephone call for Mr. Deane—a lady speaking from Cannes. Grateful for the fact that science did not yet enable Miss West to see him as well as hear him, Mr. Deane descended the stairs sleepily after the briefest of toilets.

"Gladys speaking. I was at Monte Carlo last night with some Americans, and in the Rooms I saw a lady I had last seen in London at the hotel which we so often talk about. She had room number twelve there. You remember her, too, don't you?"

"Perfectly. What was she doing when you caught sight of her?"

A little gurgle came through. "Talking to Jack."

"Indeed!" Pointer's voice sounded as amused as hers, but his eyes were hard and keen. "Oh, indeed! Had she got rid of her cold?"

"You'll have to ask him. I was miles away from them, stuck in a block of people around one of the tables. But it seems that Jack was only telling her the way out."

"You saw him later on?"

"No. He too had vanished by the time I got clear. You see, he didn't expect me there. I had tried to 'phone him, but he was out all day. But I got through to him the first thing this morning."

Pointer's free hand gave an impatient tap to the table.

"Bless all amateurs!" he would have liked to reply, but he changed it instead to "I see. But first about yourself. You didn't notice where Miss—umph—"

"Twelve went to?"

"No, I only saw her for the one second, but I thought

you'd be interested."

"Quite right. How was she dressed?"

"Beautifully, I guess. I can't get used to people leaving all their clothes behind them, but she had as much on as the wife of one of your ambassadors who was there, too, and Miss Les—Twelve had the finer jewels."

"Did Mr. Crane have anything interesting to tell you about her?"

"Oh, no, he was merely watching a table when she asked him the way out. She was standing beside him you see, and as she really was a lady, and alone, and had got separated from her husband, why, of course, he showed her the way out himself. In the vestibule sure enough was the husband, and they went off together. John had had enough of the rooms—and isn't the air hot inside—so he roamed along the *terasse*—you know what a wonderful night it was, and then after supper at the Paris motored back to Nice. But say now, Mr. Deane, don't you want to come and have a nice long talk with me, or have me come and see you? I'm so dull here."

There was nothing she could do yet, Pointer assured her, by which he meant that there was nothing he wanted her to do, and remained adamant in spite of all her appeals. His next 'phone was to Watts to come immediately to the hotel. Then he rang up Carter, who having a 'phone beside his bed answered at once, but apparently he could add nothing to Miss West's account. Until Christine had 'phoned him half an hour before he had had no idea as to who the lady was who had spoken to him last night at the Monte Carlo Rooms. Her husband was a smart, youngish-looking man with something military about his get-up. Where the couple went to Carter did not try to see.

Toule, the French detective "attached" to Carter, when questioned next on the 'phone, only knew that "Mr. Crane" had taken a car from the hotel and driven along the Corniche road to Monte Carlo, returning late at night—about twelve the hotel-porter said.

"Humph!" was the only comment of Mr. Deane as he returned to his room, where Watts was already waiting.

"Watts, get off to Monte Carlo at once. Miss West saw Miss Leslie and Carter talking together in the Rooms there last night. His explanation is"—the Chief Inspector repeated the conversations. "You have a snapshot of her—" The ladies occupying both No. 12 and No. 11 of the Enterprise had been snapshotted going down the hotel steps on the Monday following the discovery of "Eames' suicide." "Rake the coast from Ventimiglia to Marseilles if you have to, but get on her track. What will you go as?"

"Colonel Hunter," Watts said gloomily. He disliked that gentleman exceedingly, from his walrus moustache to his political opinions, and his miserable golf handicap, but it was his best impersonation, and the only one for which he had a passport.

"Right."

The future Colonel bustled off after making a note or two. He did not report for a couple of days, and then he called up Pointer to say that Captain and Mrs. Anstruther were also stopping at the Negresco, where, oddly enough, they had gone from the Hermitage, the afternoon after the lady was seen talking to Carter. In the hotel a slight, casual-looking acquaintance seemed to have been struck up between them and Carter, ostensibly connected with his civility to Mrs. Anstruther at Monte Carlo. The closest watching had as yet shown nothing suspicious beyond the facts themselves.

Within the hour a tall, dark-haired, black-moustached man sent in his name to Mrs. Anstruther as one of the *Daily Post's* reporters.

It was Captain Anstruther who came down into the lounge instead.

"My wife does not care to be interviewed," he said shortly, handing back his card to "Mr. Wiley." "We are at a loss to understand why she should be singled out for the favour."

"It's about her contract at the Columbine," the

journalist said chattily, "but you might do as well. The D. P. wants to know what has become of Miss Leslie and—"

"Come upstairs." Captain Anstruther spoke with more haste than hospitality. "I don't know how you got on to the fact that my wife was Miss Leslie. . . ."

"Recognised her."

"Well, you tell your paper that she's retired into private life. Look here, it's worth our while to make it worth *your* while to mention no names. See?"

"I do. But our paper thinks she married a Mr. Black, of Richmond,—or no, another place on the river—"

Captain Anstruther looked still more vexed.

"Of all the damned spying!—I'm a nephew of those Blacks as a matter of fact. Look here, keep all names out of the papers"—he squeezed a note into the journalist's hand, who returned it promptly.

"I should get the sack if I tried that game. I can keep all names out—possibly—without palm-oil. It's her broken contract anyway that our paper's keen on. Why wasn't she sued? And why no announcement of the wedding?"

Captain Anstruther bit his lip.

"Look here, Wiley, you seem a decent chap. I'll, well— I'll take you into our confidence. I'm divorced from my first wife, and Miss Leslie's people are Romans and fearfully pie. They'd have a fit. So, as they're buried alive in Cumberland, they'll never know—at least till the honeymoon is over—unless some paper spreads it broadcast. As to the contract—I squared the management under a pledge of the strictest secrecy. Now then, have a drink, and see how little you can tell about us, there's a good chap. You might let me see your article if you would?"

The journalist sipped his tumbler of lemonade.

"Look here," he said impulsively, "I'll scratch the whole item. I've always admired Miss Leslie immensely. I wouldn't for the world do anything to annoy her. But I wonder if she wouldn't do us instead an article on 'How it feels to be on the Stage,' or some 'Reminiscences.' She could sign her old name to them all right."

"I'll bring her in and you can ask her yourself."

Miss Leslie was quite taken with the idea of a fortnightly article.

The first one on "Hardships of the dressing-room" would let her fire off quite a few burning truths she had often wished to singe the manager with in the days of her comparative poverty. And it would keep her people quiet.

Mr. Wiley only stipulated that the articles should be sent through him, and that he must, of course, be kept in touch with the authoress until the series of six articles for which he contracted in the name of his paper was finished. The Anstruthers, who knew nothing of the newspaper world, were quite impressed by Mr. Wiley's ability and helpful suggestions, and he left the apartment with their permanent address in his pocket.

He walked back to the Chief Inspector's hotel, whence a 'phone to Watts relieved that detective of some of his anxiety, for to watch a person with a known address is a very different job than keeping an eye on a homeless wanderer who may vanish utterly within a quarter of an hour. A telegram to the Yard brought the confirmation of the marriage, the bride's Roman Catholic parents in Cumberland, and of the husband's large estates in Devon. Of the lady herself Pointer had a mixed impression. On the whole he pigeon-holed her as belonging to those women who, outwardly well bred, can be swung completely off their balance by but one force —the power of money. She struck him as a woman determined to have her share—and as much more perhaps as she could compass—of the good things of life. He took her husband to be of different calibre, and in his case the incentive of a possible need of money would be absent. So she had married a relation of the young fellow she had braved the rain storm on that August Saturday to see. He had not turned up, and whatever the reason the Chief Inspector wondered idly whether Black ever knew that it was his absence which had cost him the lady's affections.

On the evening of the next day arrived the key from Barcelona—the key which he hoped would successfully unlock the Aglae safe in the villa.

At Nice there is some society function every night during the season. This night it was a big ball in honour of a Spanish prince at Baron Boron's castle on its beautiful hill. All the Riviera world would be there. He and Watts, taken off duty temporarily, watched the departure of the motor containing Mrs. Erskine, the Clarks, and Major Vaughan. Leaving the other man near the gate to give an alarm, if need should arise, Pointer, after allowing the servants time to be gathered comfortably around the supper table, mounted a ladder as once before; but this time it was a silk one, which he lifted over the sill once he had entered by Mrs. Erskine's window, which stood open, for the night was warm. The door safely bolted, the Chief Inspector approached the safe and disconnected the alarums. Even his heart beat faster as he inserted the Foch key. It turned easily, the door swung open, and with a deep breath the police-officer took off his hat mentally to Foch as he looked inside.

Three hours later he touched Watts on the shoulder, and leaving him to taxi back to the Negreso, where Mr. Crane was among the "not-invited," Pointer sent off a pile of telegrams to all the air-stations near London.

The replies drifted in next day. Among them was an answer to an earlier request for information concerning Major Vaughan. That officer had distinguished himself on several occasions during the Great War, and it was a matter of comment that he had not received either the Military or the Victoria Cross which had been as good as promised him. His means were believed to be small. He had not returned to London for many years now, and was reported to suffer from weak lungs, which needed Riviera sunshine.

M. Guillaume of the Prefecture knew nothing against

the major, any more than he did against the Clarks. All three seemed to the French police to be model Riviera guests, wealthy, well-born, and entertaining a good deal. Only the major's health was not up to the rest of his report. It sometimes necessitated seclusions for a week at a time in his charming bachelor flat, but Pointer agreed that this could hardly be considered a moral blemish. He walked along the Promenade des Anglais to think it all out. But in vain did the azure arms of land bend around one of the loveliest bays in the world, a sea of cobalt and violet and silver. In vain did sunshine, African in its splendour, beat on him. The Chief Inspector's thoughts were brooding on too black a crime to take their hue from Nature. Though he strolled under the palm trees beside beds of nodding cyclamen, in reality he walked only along a twisted, tortuous murder trail, which still baffled him. Now and again he faced the casino, rising from the sea with gilded cupolas and airy pinnacles like a fairy palace, but he saw ever instead a young man's dead face—and a wardrobe—and a poison draught—and motives obscure and dark.

He decided to start that night for Biarritz. Since he could not pick up the ends of the threads here, he might chance on them further back in the surroundings of the widow years before she moved to this side of France. Colonel Hunter he left to hover around Carter, in spite of Watts' hints that the villa might yield a better harvest to an unobtrusive investigator.

"I've arranged that with Guillaume at the Prefecture. A hint that Mrs. Erskine may possibly be in some danger, which I hope to locate shortly, will keep her safe. Not that I anticipate any trouble. As for you, shadow Carter closely, and trail him if he leaves Nice." A few directions followed as to where, and when, to communicate with himself; and Watts, willy-nilly, had to readjust Colonel Hunter's buttonhole and, stroking that warrior's moustache firmer into place, descend the stairs, meditating on the charms of a farm in Canada, or a free life in Australia, careers for which he had as much talent or real liking as a mole might have for catching birds.

Pointer found Mrs. Erskine's circle in Biarritz almost impossible to reconstruct after fifteen years. However, he at last unrolled the main outlines to where she had left to spend the summer on a farm further in the Pyrenees. Here the path seemed to end, till an idea came to him. A library! Especially a circulating library with English books! He found the only one in Biarritz. The manager told him he had kept it over thirty years. Did he have all books entered? Naturally, the owner in Paris was most particular. Could he trace any library books which might have been sent out to No. 42, Avenue de Paris, fifteen years ago? He could, but he did not look enchanted at the prospect, until Pointer begged him to use the trifle he pressed into his hand to buy himself some cigars. Next morning the police-officer got his money's worth. The manager had found three entries fifteen years ago to a Mrs. Erskine, but the books had not been sent to the address the Chief Inspector had given, but to a farm near St. Jean de Luz. Pointer taxied at once to the place. It was still in the same hands, and Monsieur Jaureguibarry recognised the portrait of Mrs. Erskine, but knew none of her friends, except her companion, though he could not remember that lady's name. His visitor's book gave Paris as the objective of the two ladies on leaving the Basque farm.

"Paris," mused Pointer. He hoped that she had made some stop on the way, and, allowing for the length of the journey from the farm, he decided to try Bayonne as the first likely place. He had guessed rightly, and found Mrs. Erskine's name on an old register of the Grand Hotel. She seemed to have made a stay of over three weeks there, and he sallied out on his round of questions once more. First of all was a telegram to Russell asking for all details in full of any "companions" Mrs. Erskine had ever had, and what had become of them. The reply arrived after a little delay.

"We know only of two women who acted as companions to Mrs. Erskine. First a Scotswoman, Janet Fraser by name, whom she mentions once in a letter about a year after her husband's death. She is dead. Then in a mortgage executed by Mrs. Erskine some four years later as a witness to her signature we have an entry of 'Mabel Baker. Companion to Mrs. Erskine.' Am posting document to you.

Mabel Baker! Mabel— Pointer's eyes snapped. The passport of Mrs. Clark found in the safe at the villa did not give her maiden name, but he had written to the passport office for the particulars furnished by her when applying for it. On her application form she had entered her name as Mabel Baker, daughter of Arthur Baker, of Norwich. He had tried unsuccessfully to find out anything about Arthur Baker, the father, and all that he knew of herself and her husband was that their forms had been signed by their London bank-manager, who was unable after so many years to furnish any particulars Their address was a house in Kensington which had long ago been converted into flats, so that all efforts to trace the couple further back or further forward had failed, but here at last was a new fact that fitted a theory of Robert Erskine's murder, which since the night when Foch's key had opened the safe had been steadily accumulating weight in his mind.

Christine felt more and more disappointed as the weeks passed and no sign came from Pointer. Nothing seemed to be being done. He had spoken of spade work, but she feared that the police had dug themselves in, and that valuable time was being lost. She even began to doubt their keenness. After all it was they who had actually blundered so far as to imprison her John. Might they not be off on some other equally wild-goose chase? Carter preached patience at their weekly meetings, but he could not hide his surprise at the slowness of the official tempo. Pointer would have been grimly amused could he have heard them. The two young people talked in odd *confiseries* or took excursions together, meeting "by chance" in the tram, and having lunch "by chance" in the same inns, with a tea also by the same coincidence in the same cake-shop, or on the same hotel verandah. Luck, however, never favoured them to such an extent that they were quite alone. Some man, now old, now young, now middle-aged, was sure to be already there, or come in with them, or enter before they were more than seated. It never occurred to Christine that the faithful Watts was on duty, and that a great deal more than she would have cared for was absorbed by his attentive ears.

One day, when the Chief Inspector had been close on a fortnight away, Carter watched Christine get down from the tram and pass in through the doors of the Galeries Lafayette. They had already said good-bye for another week before boarding the tram at the top of the hill, but he watched her, thinking that there was no gait in the world to touch hers. Christine had decided that new gloves were a necessity even though the question of clothes did not interest her at all in these dark days. While she was trying on a pair, a voice, low and faintly monotonous, spoke to her. It was Mrs. Erskine. She asked Christine to come back to the villa for tea. The girl accepted at once, for she hoped to hear that Pointer after all had been making some fresh discovery, of which the mother had been kept informed. But Mrs. Erskine had nothing to tell her, as she complained during the drive back, and both women lamented the proverbial stupidity of Scotland Yard. The Scots-woman asked Christine to pass on at once into the *loggia* used for tea on warm days, while she took off her things. The *loggia* was a pretty spot, with well-placed mirrors duplicating the scenery, and gay with tubs of flowering plants. There were a couple of rows of books running around its three sides, and Christine idly picked up a Paris guide. It belonged, as she saw by the name in it, to Mrs. Clark. A loose sheet of letterpaper fell out as she turned it over. It was the first half-sheet of a letter. Christine's eyes grew larger. It was in Robert's handwriting,—a letter to his mother—a Christmas letter dated four years back. She stiffened. Over and over again she read the words, they were the ones which had disagreeably struck the Chief Inspector in Paris. Christine folded the half-sheet carefully away. Mrs. Erskine had tea alone with her. There was evidently a bridge party going on below. She tried to continue their conversation of the car about the impasse in her son's "case," but Christine let each question drop until her hostess had had some tea. She was anxious that the shock of what she had to say should not be too much for one whose health was so delicate. When the tea-things had been cleared away, she spoke slowly.

"I *have* got something I should like to say about Rob's case, but could I talk it over with you in your boudoir? This is such an open place."

Mrs. Erskine looked at her very keenly. In silence she led the way, and closed the door behind her visitor.

Christine held out the half-sheet of note-paper. "This dropped out of a book of Mrs. Clark's I happened to pick up while waiting for you just now."

Mrs. Erskine put on her glasses. Her hand went out in a sudden nervous little jerk. "One of my Robert's letters! Oh, let me have it! I thought I had lost them all!"

Christine gauged the mother's affection by the eagerness of the voice and eyes. She had never seen Mrs. Erskine show her heart so clearly, and her own went out warmly to the widowed, childless woman before her.

"Mrs. Erskine," Christine moistened her lips, "there's been a strange mistake somewhere. That looks like a letter from Robert, but it isn't! He never wrote those lines. Never!"

"What?" Mrs. Erskine turned very pale—"what do you mean?" The half-sheet which she held in her hand shook till Christine wondered that it did not rattle.

"You see, *I* wrote Rob's Christmas letter for him four years ago. He had burnt his hand badly at the mills, and couldn't go anywhere, so that we had a quiet time together, like old times. He dictated a letter to you and I wrote it. Jack can tell you the same thing. Besides, you might have known that Rob couldn't— wouldn't have written like that."

Mrs. Erskine Seemed dazed. "But—but—they were all alike. All his letters were the same. . . . And who's Jack?"

"A friend of mine who used to know Rob well—in Canada. I'm so sorry to've sprung this on you, but you ought to know it, and at least you can comfort yourself with the thought that your son never wrote such horrible letters as you have been thinking all these years. Surely someone with you must have had a motive to intercept your son's letters, and forge others in their stead."

"It's his paper—the paper he always used." Mrs. Erskine seemed quite dazed. She gave Christine the impression of a woman speaking in a nightmare.

"It may be, but it's not his letter. You see, I happen to be in a position to swear to that one, and to prove it in time. Lots of other people knew of his accident. Now, Mrs. Erskine, who is there who could have done so wicked, so cruel a thing?"

Mrs. Erskine suddenly got up, as though she found the room stifling. She looked ghastly, and to Christine she looked frightened as well.

"I must be alone—this shock—this blow—I want time"—she held out a cold, shaking hand—"will you come back—it's now five. Will you come back at seven without fail? Without fail? I—promise me you won't speak of this to anyone in the meanwhile. I know a French detective, not so far from here, before whom I want to lay the case. He is the only man who can solve this riddle. But I'll go into that later when you come back. Promise that you won't speak of it to anyone in the meanwhile. I have a feeling that absolute secrecy is essential if this mystery is to be unravelled,—and unravelled it must be—and quickly!"

Christine would have taken the widow's hand, but Mrs. Erskine did not see her gesture. There was

something fierce in her eyes. Action, not sentiment, was
evidently rising rapidly in her heart to the exclusion of
any softer feeling. Christine mentally apologised to her
for ever having thought her dull and cold.

"But what about the Inspector?" she asked gently.

"You mean yon English policeman? That dolt has done
nothing but muddle and muddle along. And where is he
now? Away on his holidays, I shouldna be surprised."

Christine made a little deprecatory *moue.*

"Still, the case is in his hands," she ventured, and
remembering how he had come to the help of them all at
Lille, she repeated more firmly. I do think you owe it to
him to let him know about this at once."

"And where is he to be found?" Mrs. Erskine asked
fiercely; "tell me that?"

Christine had not the faintest idea, and said so. She
could not add that the Chief Inspector had told her to
consult Mr. Watts should any emergency arise while he
was away.

Mrs. Erskine sank back into her chair. "He bade me
'phone to the Prefecture if anything unexpected should
happen, and it's aye the unexpected to that man that
happens in all his cases, I'm thinking. Well, instead of the
Prefecture, I am going, as I told you, to employ a most
clever French detective of whose skill I've had some verra
good proofs indeed in other days. Now, Christine, my
dear"—she had never called the girl that before—"just
send a wire, or a letter, to your *pension* in Cannes and
bide the night here with me. I have much to do. I need
you. Leave me to myself now, but come you back at seven
without fail and we will see what my Frenchman can do
to clear up this dreadful discovery of yours." Mrs. Erskine
was deeply moved. She folded one trembling hand over
the other, as though to keep them quiet by force.

"I canna believe it"—she turned her glowing eyes on
the girl—"I canna yet believe what you've told me. To-
night you must let me hear anything that you remember
from my Rob's letters. The letters that I never received."

Mrs. Erskine covered her face with her hands, and only made a gesture of farewell as Christine passed her.

"Don't fail me!" she breathed, and the girl laid a tender hand for a second on the bowed shoulder.

She herself spent the interval as in a dream. What did it mean? What could it mean? Was there really someone in the house with Mrs. Erskine who had substituted those brutal begging letters; but how had they been able to profit by the money? Surely there could not have been an accomplice at the other end as well? Someone who could take Mrs. Erskine's letters with their money contents and change them again for the cold, formal epistles which alone had reached Rob? Yet he had been allowed to receive the thousand pounds! Christine felt her head in a whirl, and she tried to think of something else as she walked by the sea. There was something, too, in Mrs. Erskine's manner which suggested that she knew more than she would admit. She was afraid of something, or someone. What or who? Christine was thankful that the mother could turn to an expert who could throw daylight on what seemed so dark, and to whom the other would at last speak out.

It was not quite seven when she returned to the villa.

It was on the afternoon of the same day that Pointer set out for Nice. He 'phoned to Christine from Marseilles, where the train had a wait. The puzzle had yielded to the key. He knew now the truth about Robert Erskine's murder, but he wanted her help with regard to his letters to his mother.

The Chief Inspector was told that mademoiselle was out, but would be back in the afternoon. A 'phone to the Negresco informed him that Crane was away too. He wondered if he had struck the weekly meeting day of the young couple, and left a message for Christine to expect a 'phone from Nice at the hour when his train arrived. A few words over the instrument would tell him all that he wanted to know. To "Colonel Hunter" he wired instructions to meet Mr. Deane at the station.

Watts met him, but it seemed that Miss West had not yet returned to her *pension*. Not only that, but she had 'phoned about an hour ago to say that she was spending the night in Nice with friends, and would possibly be away a day or two. "Yes, mademoiselle had sent the 'phone herself."

"The devil!" murmured Pointer thoughtfully; "that can only mean she's at the villa! The very devil! Where's Carter?" he asked aloud of Watts, who as yet had heard nothing concerning the other's journey.

"He is to dine with the Anstruthers to-night. When I left he was playing tennis with one of the Chapman boys."

"Humph!" grunted Pointer, "we'll try to get him."

Carter's voice answered him at once.

"Hello! That you, Deane? At last! Anything turned up? What? Where's Miss West? In Cannes. She was going back by the three-fifteen. Am I sure? No, I can't be sure, as she never lets me see her off. Orders, you know. But when I left her at half-past two that was her intention. Is anything the matter?"

"Not that I know of, but keep near the 'phone for a few minutes, will you?"

"You bet!" Pointer heard before he disconnected. He promptly rang up Mrs. Erskine. That lady, too, was out, Marie's voice informed him. Had Miss West been there during the afternoon? Yes, she had had tea with madame, and had left a little before six o'clock. No, she had not returned.

Again the Chief Inspector looked thoughtfully at his boot-tips. Watts, who knew his little ways, wondered what was worrying him. In another second Pointer was speaking to Carter again and asking him to come around to his hotel at once in the big car he hired regularly.

"For God's sake, tell me is there anything wrong with Christine," urged the Canadian; but the Chief Inspector hung up the receiver. He next tried to get into touch with the Prefecture, but the line was occupied, and before he got through Carter's car was at the door and that young man was in the room.

"Look here, you can't keep silence like this. What's, wrong? Why did you ask about Christine?"

"I'd like to know where she is," was all Pointer would reply. "She's not at her *pension;* I want to find out just where she is. Drive to the villa."

It was close on eight o'clock when the car rushed up the drive. Pierre came out at once.

"M. and Mme. Clark were out. They had left after six o'clock, he thought." He himself looked slightly dishevelled. Marie came running down from the floor above.

"Ah, I thought it *was* your voice, Monsieur Pointer! What a pity madame is out. But pray come in and rest yourselves, gentlemen." They followed her upstairs into the drawing-room.

"Major Vaughan in?" asked Pointer.

For answer she went to the little house 'phone on the wall. There was no reply to her ringing.

"He is out, and his man, too, monsieur."

"Do you know when madame will return? We must see mademoiselle as soon as possible. It is most important. She has not gone back to Cannes. We made sure that she would be spending the night here. Are you certain that she did not come back later and go out with Madame or the Clarks?"

"Ah-h, that was, of course, quite possible. As a matter of fact there had been a dreadful upset here. Madame Clark had lost the wonderful emerald pendant she values so highly."

She had discovered her loss a little before six, and after that Marie hardly knew what had happened. Pierre had been sent post haste in a taxi way out to the *Palais des Marguerites*, where Madame Clark had been last night, in case . . . It was absurd to send him, but Madame Clark and her husband, usually so gay, were quite beside themselves; even the *chef de cuisine* and the kitchen man had been made to help in the hunt,—been sent all the distance to some lunch place at Monte Carlo. Madame Clark had got Madame Erskine to send her, Marie, in a taxi to Antibes, where the Clarks had been during the late afternoon. As for Madame Clark's own maid, it was her afternoon off. Marie did not know whether the pendant had been found or not during their absence. She herself had only just got back when M. Pointer telephoned, and as for Pierre, he also was but just returned—the others were still away. But as the car was out, the Clarks were out, and madame as well as the major were out, Marie thought that the emerald must have found itself, and the household be taking its evening amusements as usual. But what a day! Oh, la, la!"

Pointer walked swiftly through the rooms of the flat, followed by Carter, silent and anxious. Watts, at a whisper, was looking over the rest of the house, beginning—thanks to his pass-key, with the major's rooms. Pointer stopped in a small dining-room Mrs. Erskine used for herself, or a very small dinner party of intimate friends.

"When was the last meal served here?"

"Not for over a week, monsieur."

Pointer asked Marie to be kind enough to 'phone to a Mr. Deane at the Moderne to join him as soon as convenient at the villa. "He is a sort of guardian of mademoiselle. If he is not in, ask them in the hotel to look for him, and kindly wait by the 'phone. He will be in shortly in any case."

Having thus got rid of her for some little time, Pointer stopped and picked up a couple of fair-sized crumbs.

"They're quite fresh. Someone's had a meal here recently." He motioned Carter to stand with his back against the door, and opened a couple of cupboards. He glanced keenly at the bottom plates of a little pile.

"Still greasy. Been wiped with a newspaper." He felt inside all the cups. "Two are quite wet." He paused over some teaspoons before he hunted on, as though for something more definite still. Finally he pounced on a crumpled little newspaper thrust into an empty cardboard box on the back of the lowest shelf. He opened this out on the table. A few scraps of bread and ham were inside. "Two people have had a meal of sorts within the hour." He shut the cupboards, whisked off the lace centre and emptied the waste-paper basket on the polished surface. More crumbs, bits of litter, and a faded flower tumbled out. Pointer pounced on this last.

"A clove carnation. Was Miss West wearing any? There are none about."

"Not when I saw her."

"Marie!" called Pointer, and the maid came running up. "Was mademoiselle wearing carnations when she came to tea?"

Marie shook her head with a smile.

"Ah, monsieur met her, then, later? I did give her a bunch when she was leaving. Mademoiselle loves them so."

Marie was quite certain that Christine had only been in the *loggia* and the boudoir during her afternoon call.

Watts, who had joined the little group, shook his head. No one was in the house. Pointer walked swiftly downstairs and out on to the drive.

"How much petrol has been taken, Pierre?" asked the Chief Inspector. "As I said, we must catch up with mademoiselle, in her own interests, to-night. It is a question of a paper she must sign. These gentlemen have come as witnesses."

Pierre rushed off to the garage. "No tin has been touched, and there was very little in the car."

Pointer stood motionless. Carter started to speak, but a glance from the police-officer's eyes stopped him. Every mental nerve of Pointer's was strung taut to the call he was making on it. Where had Christine gone or been taken? He wasted no time on speculating on the why. He looked at the tyre-tracks from the garage to the house, which showed fairly clearly in the dust.

"Those wheels wouldn't do for any hill climbing. Who generally drove the car?" he asked in French.

"Generally M. Clark. Sometimes, though rarely, M. le Majeur. Neither would try to climb with those tyres."

"And very little petrol . . . humph!" Pointer picked up the 'phone mouthpiece and called a number, adding a code word swiftly.

"'Ello! Monsieur Guillaume there, by any chance, still? Ah, Monsieur Gamier! You will do perfectly. No, it is nothing to do with my 'phone from Tarascon this morning. That matter is all arranged, thanks to your colleague, but I would like to know whether Madame Erskine owns a launch or a yacht? No? Then, will you kindly have inquiries made at once as to whether one has been hired to-day, late in the afternoon, by anyone at the villa. It is most urgent."

Pointer walked up and down, saying nothing. Carter, very pale, stared hard at him, but did not offer to speak. Watts was lost in speculation. The Chief Inspector leapt to the instrument at the bell's first premonitory tinkle.

"Yes? Ah, good! Madame Clark hired it, you say. One of the swiftest steam launches here. By 'phone about six, to await her at the harbour steps by seven? Five people in all? Three ladies—one young—and two men. That is the party. Oh, thank you, we should indeed be most grateful. There are three of us. We will be with you in a little minute, and if your surgeon could accompany us he might come in useful. I do not know what we shall find."

Carter blanched as he heard him.

Pointer turned to the other two.

"Your car, Carter! Miss West is on a launch which we shall be able to overhaul on a still faster police boat which the Prefecture puts at our disposal. We're in plenty of time." But Pointer ran down the steps and leapt up beside the driver's seat as though the margin of safety were not so wide as he had said.

A direction or two, a turn of Carter's wheel, and they

whirled up to a quiet part of the old town's harbour where lay a wicked looking little craft. A gendarme took charge of the car, they stepped aboard, and off the launch flew like an arrow through the quiet blue evening.

"So Mrs. Clark arranged this party, did she?" Pointer said with a hard stare through the lovely lilac shades of the early evening. "I fancy it will be her last pleasure jaunt for some time."

"What is it you're afraid of, in Heaven's name?" Carter asked, as so often before; but Pointer only shook his head.

"Too complicated to explain just now. I think we shall be in plenty of time."

CHAPTER ELEVEN

"Is Mrs. Erskine in any danger, too?" Watts ventured in an aside as the boat cut through the smooth water.

"In very grave danger, indeed, I fancy."

"And shall I still keep an eye on him?" "Him" was Carter, staring ahead of the two police-officers.

"You won't need to, after to-night," was the oracular reply.

"There she is!" Carter called suddenly. "There's the large steam launch you described."

He was right. It was the *Hirondelle*, the boat that Mrs. Clark had hired. Pointer, once he knew that she was the one they wanted, hardly glanced at her: his eyes were fixed on a black stretch of water, beyond a projecting arm of land, which lay sombre and unlit.

"Catch her up before she reaches that."

"The 'Devil's Sock,' as our smugglers call it? *Bien*. We shall do it."

And they did. The launch when hailed stopped instantly.

"Who is it?" called Clark's breezy voice, in his bad French. "Anything wrong? Can we help?"

The police cutter closed up. In the light of its electric lamps the face talking to them changed suddenly, the jaw slackened, the eyes darted furtively from the police-boat to the pleasure craft about, who were watching the meeting with curiosity.

"It's all right, Mr. Clark," the Chief Inspector answered civilly as he mounted the ladder swiftly, followed by Carter and Watts. "Only Miss West is most urgently wanted, and we heard that she had gone out with you in the swiftest launch in Nice, so I borrowed a police-cutter." He had opened the door of the little cabin as he spoke. Carter would have pushed in first if the other's sheer bulk had not prevented it. As for Watts, a glance from Pointer made him wait outside.

In the unusually large and airy cabin sat the three other occupants of the villa and Christine. The women lay back in their chairs with closed eyes as though asleep; only Major Vaughan blinked evilly at them.

"Christine!" Carter fell on his knees beside her. "Christine!" He shook her gently. "She's unconscious. Give me some brandy—some coffee." His gaze swept the table doubtfully.

Pointer said something over the rail, and a man stepped up on to the deck.

"Here is the surgeon. He'll soon tell us if anything serious is the matter."

The doctor rolled up Christine's eyelid, felt her pulse, and poured her out some brandy from his flask. He looked at a coffee-tray on the table, smelt the coffee, tasted it, and added his brandy to a cup of the steaming beverage. "She'll be all right with as much of that as you can get her to drink."

He bent over the other two women. "Same here. Opium den, eh?" He whispered to Pointer, who nodded.

A French sergeant of police stepped in, curled his moustache fiercely, and made a few notes in a book.

"You will all accompany me to the police-station for inquiries on arrival in the harbour."

The major cackled softly.

"Why? The ladies would try a little dose of my Eastern friend. I told them beginners should go slow."

"*Il n'y' a pas d'explications!*" snapped the Frenchman, seating himself between the two men, while Watts lounged against the door. Christine opened her eyes drowsily,' and closed them after a look of infinite relief as she saw Carter's face bending over her. Another sip or two, and she was able to stagger outside, and supported by Carter and the doctor walk up and down in the fresh air.

"Where's Mrs. Erskine—Mrs. Erskine's in danger," she suddenly babbled after her second cup. "And I thought I saw Mr. Pointer—"

"Here I am, Miss Christine," came the cheery answer as the Chief Inspector relieved the doctor, who returned to the cabin to look after the other two ladies.

"Oh, Mr. Pointer!" Christine clutched the cup he held out to her dizzily.

"I—there's a letter Mrs. Erskine has which Rob never wrote—someone's deceived her all these years. He never wrote any of them." She tried to speak coherently. Pointer pressed her arm soothingly.

"I know. Don't you worry, Miss West. You let Carter take you home and sleep this off till he calls for you in the morning."

"But Mrs. Erskine—those horrible men—Mrs. Erskine—"

"She's quite safe now. Watts is in the cabin. I shall stay with her, and when Carter has seen you safely into Madame Secret's hands at my hotel—she's plenty of empty rooms—he'll join me, and between us Mrs. Erskine will be well taken care of, don't you think so yourself?"

Christine could not think yet. Her mind could only give out the impressions made on it while it was still working normally before she had taken the drug. She drank some more coffee at Carter's urgence.

"Are we making for *Californie?* Surely we ought to be there by now."

"Californie, eh? Why Californie?" asked Pointer.

"Mrs. Erskine's friend—no, not a friend,—a man she knows—a detective—lives there. We're taking Rob's letter to him—he's very clever, or something. . . ."

"You found Robert Erskine's letter when you went to tea at the villa, didn't you?"

In vain Carter gave the Chief Inspector a look not to worry Christine just now. Pointer thought it did her as much good to exercise her brains as her lungs, once he saw that she was physically up to the exertion.

"Yes. Has she told you? Oh, thank Heaven you both came."

Carter could keep silence no longer.

"Christine, darling, who gave you that stuff to drink?"

"I didn't drink it. She moved her arm as though it pained her. I—"

"What happened when you got back at seven?" asked Pointer.

Christine struggled bravely to answer, and what with the coffee and brandy, and her own desire to speak, the effort grew easier after the first broken gasps.

"At seven? Oh, yes, something had upset the household. There didn't seem to be any servants—we had to wait on ourselves—and when we got to the garage Pierre wasn't there—Mrs. Erskine had counted on getting away unnoticed—by ourselves. But Mr. Clark heard us talking and dragged it out of her that we were off for Californie. So he insisted on our letting him drive us there down to a launch his wife and the major were waiting in and going to Californie by water. I felt horrid when I stepped on board. If only I could have drawn back I would, but I couldn't leave Mrs. Erskine. Besides, I wanted to see the affair cleared up as much as she did, only I sure hated coming on this yacht. I leant over the rails here and refused to go into the cabin where the others went to play bridge. I seemed to suddenly see us two or perhaps three—I don't know about Mrs. Clark—I wondered what sort of people they all really were, for I felt that Mrs. Erskine distrusted them, too, since she knew about those letters. I began to think about Rob. Next Mr. Clark came away from the engine over there and the major came out of the cabin. They stood on both sides of me, and Mr. Clark made some remark about the view. And all of a sudden I felt frightened. Jack, what I would have given to have had you there!"—Jack pressed her arm —"I stepped back from between them, but Mr. Clark —to think that I used to rather like him—caught me and held me tight while the major ran something hard into my arm. It hurt frightfully, but Mr. Clark held me with my face pressed right into his shoulder so that I couldn't make a sound, and when he left me go and went to the engine again, the major stood in front of me and laughed."

"He won't laugh next time he sees you, and as for Clark—" Carter spoke slowly between his teeth.

"I thought of Mrs. Erskine alone in the cabin—and of her revolver. I got into the cabin somehow, though my feet seemed to be made of lead, I remember her helping me to a chair, and asking what was the matter, and the next thing I heard was your voice, Jack, from miles and miles away calling to me."

Pointer thoughtfully stepped away for a moment to glance into the cabin. Mrs. Erskine, whose eyes were half open, made him a feeble sign, but he only shook his head with a gesture that implied there was no hurry, and made Christine go over the details of the afternoon again.

At the landing stage Watts helped Mrs. Erskine into a taxi, and drove her off to the villa. Pointer himself, Mrs. Clark, and the men of the party walking to the police station close at hand, while Carter took Christine to the Chief Inspector's hotel, where a sympathetic maid and landlady diagnosed her case as an attack of seasickness and helped her to bed. Carter left her door reluctantly, he would have liked to stand on guard all night after what had so nearly happened, but a confidence in Pointer was beginning to reassure him where it was a question of that police-officer's orders. At the villa he found the servants flitting uneasily about, like bats. They connected all these strange goings on with the loss of the emerald pendant and were in secret mutiny. Carter was asked to join Monsieur Pointer in the drawing-room, where he found only Mrs. Erskine lying on the chaise-lounge looking very ill, and Watts.

Pointer was just laying down a packet of legal-looking papers on the table beside her.

"Here they are. Will-forms taken from the major's pocket. If you don't understand their significance, Madame; but I see you do"—for Mrs. Erskine was staring with dilated eyes at them. "It would have taken some persuasion doubtless to make you sign away your fortune to any one of your three friends, but—as I think you know—they would have ways of persuading you, and whether the will would have been valid wouldn't have interested you, once you had followed Miss West to the bottom of the Mediterranean. It would have been so easy to connect the two 'accidents.' Miss West overbalanced, and you falling over in an effort to save her. True, your friends might have had a few awkward questions to answer; but, after all, the French courts will decide on the question of the attempted murder of Miss West, that's none of my business for the moment.' Pointer took a step forward—" This is my real reason for being here to-night. Janet Fraser, you are detained, pending an extradition order, for the murder of Robert Erskine, and for the embezzlement of the Erskine funds, under false pretences for over seventeen years. It's my . . ."

There was a shriek from the woman to whom he was speaking. She sprang to her feet and looked around her as if demented, as indeed she was by the shock—for the moment.

"The devils! They've sold me! After all the money they've squeezed from me they've sold me in the end. Sold me!"

She screeched, arching her back and advancing in a horribly feline sidle.

"What else did you expect?" Pointer asked imperturbably. "But it's my duty to warn you that anything you say may be used against you."

"My God, Mrs. Erskine!" Watts murmured, while Carter felt as though the solid floor had opened under his feet.

The woman sank back on the sofa, and struggled for self-possession. "I'm drugged—I don't know what I'm saying—I drank some morphia—we all did—just to taste it for once, you know . . ." she was mouthing and grinning horribly—"and it's quite taken my senses away."

"Neither you nor Mrs. Clark got much of the stuff into your systems," Pointer said in his hard official voice; "when you two heard me on deck you each jabbed a needleful into your arms, but half of it came out again. Your wrists were all wet to the touch."

Yet as a matter of fact it was just this small amount of morphia, irritating instead of calming as a larger dose would have been, which had thrown and was throwing off its balance the cold, calculating brain of the woman whom Pointer knew was not Mrs. Erskine.

"I don't know what you're talking about." She tried again to steady her flighty wits. "Ask Mr. Russell who I am."

Carter, who was listening still as a man in a dream, saw now why the Chief Inspector had begun as he did. He had thrown the woman off her guard by fear and rage. Unstrung by the growing strain of the investigation into Robert Erskine's murder, by the morphia taken, by the revelation of how near she herself had been to the end of all things at the hands of her accomplices, she could not recover her poise, try for it as she might. Like some tight-rope walker over an abyss, she made a desperate effort to save herself even when she was already all but falling headlong. "Mr. Russell met me scores of times before my husband's death as well as since."

"He was easy to hoodwink. It was his father who had known the real Mrs. Erskine well, the younger Russell had only seen her a couple of times as a lad. But your aunt by marriage, Mrs. Fraser, of Glasgow, would only too gladly swear to you any time, as will other relations. She seemed to think that your death stopped the pressing home of some claim against you about the illegal sale of a cottage of hers. She sent me your photo. . . ."

The woman in the white wig, and artificially shaped eyebrow, bit her grey lips.

"You are Janet Fraser, of Murry Street, Glasgow. You were engaged as a companion by the late Mrs. Erskine some fifteen years ago, after having been an unsuccessful actress for over six years. You joined her near St. Jean de Luz, and went on with her to Bayonne, where she was taken with a paralytic stroke the same night and was removed to the hospital. She died a few days later without recovering consciousness. The doctor in charge of the hospital mistook you for the mistress, and you kept up the deception. He has identified the photo of Janet Fraser—your photo without that wig on, and without that shaved peak to one eyebrow. The hotel people at Bayonne and the sisters at the hospital have also identified it. Mrs. Erskine lies buried in the churchyard there under your name. We are getting an order for her exhumation under the pretext of having her body taken to Scotland. Her identity can easily be proved by a couple of operations she had had. You assumed her name, forged her hand-writing—which was a very easy one to copy. You continued to enjoy her income, until chance gave your secret away to Mrs. Clark, at that time Mabel Baker, your companion."

The woman seemed to collapse more and more as he spoke. Now she tried to pull herself up once more.

"I don't know what you're talking about," she whispered, with a voice which was but a ghost of itself.

He stopped. "Now, look here. You can deny everything, of course, but it won't help you any; and meanwhile these others, the Clarks and the major, who, I don't doubt, are as deep in it as yourself, who've battened on you for all these years, may get off scot-free, and in any case won't get much more than a few months. Do you want that?"

Her haggard eyes opened and shut themselves convulsively, her throat worked, but she forced back the words by an effort which was visible.

"Wait—I'll go on. Robert Erskine came to England. You poisoned him to prevent his discovering the fraud.

For he would have known his mother. You could not hope to always receive him in twilight as you did Mr. Russell or anyone who had ever met the real Mrs. Erskine. You wrote your letters to him as forbidding as possible in order to prevent his wanting to come to Europe and see you. But you made your big mistake when by your miserliness you only sent him one thousand pounds of the money he asked for. The whole of the five thousand would have kept him in Canada. Carter here is ready to swear that the one thousand which you finally sent him was the only money Robert Erskine ever received from you. Those letters you showed me in Paris were all forgeries. That was why you 'lost' them. You got him to supply you with a box of his stationery when you heard that he was sailing for England. The discarded box is in our possession. Unfortunately for himself, he told you that he was coming over, though he did not tell you on what business, as he had never referred to business matters with you. He gave you the name he intended to use, and you sent a letter to meet him on the boat's arrival in which you wrote of your joy at the thought of seeing him, and that he was to telegraph you as soon as he had found a hotel. He kept that letter among his papers in a safe. Otherwise you would have destroyed it as you did all the other papers in his room. But to go back, for I want you to see that there are no gaps. As soon as you knew his hotel, you flew over to England and took a room in the same house, by good luck—as you thought —getting a room very near his. You passed under the name of Mrs. Willett. You painted, padded, darkened your eyes with belladonna, and had a wig arranged to look as like a portrait of Mrs. Clark which you had with you as possible. The firm who supplied you with it, and the eyebrows meeting over the nose, kept a copy of that photo, as they always do, to safeguard themselves in case of dissatisfaction. I found an eyebrow box in the attic which bore the name of the shop."

"The others planned it. They egged me on. They were

all in it!" burst out, as though in spite of herself, from the woman. "They said it was the only way."

"Very likely they did, but, you see, I have no proofs of that. All I can prove is that when you found Robert Erskine's acquaintance impossible to make, that medicine bottle of his gave you your chance. You changed the last but one dose for a deadly solution of morphia, obtained how I can't think. . . ." Pointer knew perfectly, but he wanted her to speak, and she did.

"No, no, no! I never did such a thing!" The sane part of her brain was fighting the drugged part which wanted to babble.

"Oh, yes, you did."

"If I did, I got it from that sneering, drug-sodden fiend Vaughan."

"Robert Erskine drank the poison. When it was acting,—I take it you listened at the door—you entered his room, locked the door, unscrewed the back of the wardrobe, fastened the bolt on inside, and dragged the armchair up to it. You're a tall woman and a strong one, but you must have had some difficulty with his body before you got it safely bundled in . . ."

The woman turned livid.

". . . with your letter to the manager in the pocket. Next you laid in some things of his which you thought would bear out your 'phone about his having gone into the country, screwed the back on again, pushed the wardrobe into position, emptied the medicine bottle on to the balcony, filled in the cough mixture again, and went through all his belongings. His bag you fastened inside a larger bag. . . ."—This last was guess-work, but he saw by her terrified eyes that he had been right.— "Wearing Major Vaughan's shoes, you crept down the back stairs into the street. You had already oiled the lock and opened it at noon. When you had disposed of your bag, and exchanged the shoes for your own, you waited in the theatre and took a taxi back to the hotel. When you heard the arrival of the police—your door was ajar, we noticed—

you put on his shoes again, and crept out on to the balcony to peer in through the blind, as you had done once before when Mr. Beale was in the room. You had intended to reach France Saturday night, but the storm which raged made flight out of the question. Even the channel boats did not go. Besides, once you knew the body had been found, you waited on to see what would happen. The telegrams which I sent Mrs. Erskine here were received and answered by Mrs. Clark. You flew to Paris, using her passport, and back again the same day after the interview with Russell and me, an interview which you were expecting and had prepared for after catching sight of Mr. Russell at the hotel."

Watts shot his chief a crestfallen glance, but the woman broke out excitedly: "She lent me that passport. She helped . . . They all helped . . . They're all in it. Yes, you're right, Inspector, they knew all about it. And ever since then I've been in hell! In hell! I knew it was only a question of time before I should be killed in my turn . . . oh, my head . . . I don't mean that! I don't know what I'm saying."

"I'll just make a note of what you say about their being implicated too." Pointer drew out a block of writing paper.

She veered around again, the hatred of years sweeping away every barrier, as the wily police-officer had hoped it would. He had a full confession of the crime, written in the first person, in his pocket, only waiting for her to sign, and for that signature he was working, leaving her no time to recover that cold nerve of hers which had been temporarily broken down, but which was sure to come again later as he well knew. There was too much tension between France and England just then for extradition to be a quick matter when the crime had been committed on French soil, but with the criminal's confession safely at the Yard the police could wait in patience the law's delays.

"Stop! Write all this down." She sprang to her feet and

leant heavily against the table, rocking as she stood. "Write it all out, and I'll sign it, and then we'll see if those blood-suckers get off with only a couple of months. *Months!* While I . . ."

"You'd better see a solicitor," suggested the Chief Inspector half-heartedly, but remembering the jury's passion for every advantage to be given to the criminal, as he pulled out the sheets, which were burning his fingers.

"No, no! Is that it? Let me read it over."

"If you want to sign it, just add a line at the foot to say that you have read it through and that it is correct."

"I'll put more than that in. I want to say that these three blackmailers instigated Robert Erskine's death. They told me what to do. Ever since yon Baker found me one day asleep with my wig awry she's lived on me, she and Vaughan, who was her lover at the time, and the man she calls her husband now."

"And Miss West, what were you going to do to her?" Carter spoke for the first time—he had been literally spellbound till then. "What of her?"

For a second the woman blinked at him as though hardly remembering to whom he referred.

"I'm writing that down, too. When I told them that she had discovered something wrong with the letters— letters *they* drafted for me, mind you they insisted on drugging her, and—and—they told me that she was to be put ashore somewhere. I thought she was to be kept till we could get away safely." Her eyes flickered uneasily, and fell to the paper.

In a fury of vengeance which burned away all thought of personal safety for the moment if only she could engulf the others deep enough, Janet Fraser wrote nearly two pages before she signed her name, with Carter and Watts as witnesses.

The Chief Inspector drew a deep breath of relief, and motioned Carter to precede him out of the room.

Janet Fraser's hand went to a little picture standing

on the mantelpiece, a sketch of her father's manse. The frame was a Florentine one, and in a corner her finger pared off a tiny gilt pellet as she apparently automatically adjusted the water-colour. When Pointer turned to speak to Watts she slipped it into her mouth. It was a way of escape she had prepared long ago.

"I shall be quite ready to come with you to England without waiting for an extradition order," she said quietly as she lay down on the couch again and pulled the rug up over her, "but I'm exhausted for the moment. I want a little rest."

"Very good. I'll arrange about our tickets so that we can get off by the early train if possible. I'll be back within an hour and let you know what has been settled. There will be Watts on duty outside, but I think you'll be sensible."

"Quite sensible," murmured Janet Fraser, looking him full in the face for a second, and then dropping those pale grey eyes of hers.

Carter and the Chief Inspector walked away in silence. At last the Canadian spoke.

"So it wasn't Beale after all, and Rob was murdered by that she-devil who passed as his mother because he would have given the show away! I'm glad you got her! God! I never thought I should like to see a woman arrested for murder, but I'm glad you got her! And, see here, Inspector, I do see why you weren't keen on my helping, nor Christine either: it did take a mighty keen eye—a trained one—to pick out the king-log from that jumble."

"Largely a matter of routine," muttered Pointer, lighting his pipe.

"Routine!" Carter echoed. "I suppose it was routine that lets Christine sleep safely in her bed to-night. Poor old Rob. To be done in like that. . . . I wish to Heaven . . ." He was silent for a few minutes. "But how in tarnation did you get hold of—of—the truth?"

"Well, it's a longish story. First of all, as I said, was

that letter this woman wrote to Erskine which we found among the papers Beale had got hold of—she had destroyed the others, you know—asking him to let her know his address in London at once. That only bewildered me. You don't suspect a mother easily of having a hand in her son's murder, but I began to wonder whether Robert Erskine might turn out not to be her son at all. I found that that was impossible, and I began speculating a bit along the lines of the truth. A Toronto stationery box I found in her attic here made me doubt whether the letters I had taken a bit for granted, I confess, were as genuine as they looked. I had noted the water-mark, but had let them go at that, under the circumstances—my mistake that! Then— well, what with one thing and another, I got hold of a key to her safe and that unlocked her story as well, or at least the clue to it. It was this way. In the safe were a couple of the real Mrs. Erskine's old diaries, a large photo of herself, a small razor, and a couple of white wigs. Strange things for a lady to keep with her jewels, eh? The photo set me thinking. It had been constantly handled, and had a clip fastened to the top to allow of its being hung on any convenient nail. But why? Taken in conjunction with the wigs, why else than to make up like it? Then the little razor—Mrs. Erskine's queer eyebrow would fit that idea. In Janet Fraser's photo—I only got it later on, of course; didn't know of her existence then—you'll see what beetling eyebrows she has by nature. The two women were otherwise about the same size and general build. With the wig, and the eyebrow shaved to a peak in the middle, and after years of semi-invalidism, the one could easily pass herself off for the other, when there were no suspicions alert. I found in my hunt at the villa an old pill-box which gave me a Biarritz address, and went there. The rest of the story . . .? Well, after that it was—"

"Merely a matter of routine," suggested Carter; "but say, Chief Inspector, I'll never forget what I owe you. You saved me once when you drew Beale's fangs, and you've saved Christine to-night."

"I don't mind telling you that I never in all my life spent a worse five minutes than when I had to decide what had become of her, and knew that if I made a mistake there would be no time to put it right." Pointer spoke with feeling.

"What made you guess the river?" Carter asked in a hushed voice.

"Couldn't see what else they could do with her. It was obvious that the house had been cleared so that no one should know of her second arrival. When she had been at the villa before, she had practically no friends on this side of the Atlantic. I think they counted on that a bit. I know this coast pretty well. As Mr. Deane, I've walked it over for hours, and I couldn't call to mind any ravine or place where a body could be dropped as though from a motor accident except some spots a good way off, and where a very stiff gradient had to be climbed. The tyres and the small amount of petrol were against them. There only remained the sea, for the villa itself was out of the question. What they wanted was an accident, not a body that could be found some time or other, and prove it to've been a murder."

"You jumped to the conclusion at once that her life was in danger, then?"

Pointer put his head on one side. "Well . . . in a murder case there generally comes a moment when a second murder seems the only way to keep the first one quiet."

The two men stopped at the Negresco, and Pointer glanced up at the purple roofs high above them.

"Don't let yourself feel too grateful, Mr. Carter. You and Miss Leslie, as was, quite tangled me up for a while. There were weeks when I felt none too sure of either of you."

"See here," Carter stopped him as he would have turned away, "I saw that man of yours—Watts—pull out a knife to-night to sharpen a pencil. My knife! I had lent it to a funny old gheezer here, a Colonel Winter, who's pestered me the last fortnight, buzzing around me, and I've been kind of figuring—"

But the Chief Inspector was gone. Carter gazed after him. "Well, I guess our British police take some beating after all." And he went upstairs to write out a wire offering a reward of five thousand pounds to anyone who should first find the murderer of Robert Erskine. The wire was sent off to the Yard, after a futile effort on his part to get it dated earlier in the day. He thought it would look more natural to Pointer, but he consoled himself afterwards with the knowledge that it would have made no difference in the Chief Inspector's acceptance of the sum solely on behalf of the Police Widows' and Orphans' Fund.

When Pointer returned to the villa it was close on dawn. He and Watts looked at each other in silence a moment and then glanced away.

"A letter must have come for Mrs. Erskine late last night. I found it in the letter-box." Watts handed it to his superior.

"Any sound from in there?" asked Pointer rather tensely.

Watts shook his head, and, receiving no answer to their knock, they entered.

She was quite dead. Gone by the same way that she had sent Robert Erskine out of life. They 'phoned for a doctor, though there was no slightest chance of rousing her to life. Then Pointer glanced at the letter he held. It was from Russell and Son. He broke the seal and read:

"Dear Mrs. Erskine,
I will reply to your last at full length to-morrow. This is simply to ask you to let me have all possible details as to the death of your one-time companion, Janet Fraser. Place of burial, doctor who attended her, etc. A relative of hers has died in Australia, and as next-of-kin she—had she lived— would have inherited his enormous fortune, which

will now go to his more distant kin.

I note in your letter that your press for the sale of your Bell shares, against which we most strongly counsel you"

Pointer put the letter down for a moment, and looked thoughtfully at the dead woman before him.

THE END

Other Resurrected Press Books in *The Chief Inspector Pointer Mystery* Series

The Eames-Erskine Case
The Footsteps that Stopped
The Clifford Affair
The Cluny Problem
The Craig Poisoning Mystery
The Tall House Mystery
Tragedy at Beechcroft
The Case of the Two Pearl Necklaces
Mystery at the Rectory
Scarecrow

Murder at Bridge

When an afternoon bridge party attended by some of Hamilton's leading citizens ends with the hostess being murdered in her boudoir, Special Investigator Dundee of the District Attorney's office is called in. But one of the attendees is guilty? There are plenty of suspects: the victim's former lover, her current suitor, the retired judge who is being blackmailed, the victim's maid who had been horribly disfigured accidentally by the murdered woman, or any of the women who's husbands had flirted with the victim. Or was she murdered by an outsider whose motive had nothing to do with the town of Hamilton. Find the answer in . . . **Murder at Bridge**

One Drop of Blood

When Dr. Koenig, head of Mayfield Sanitarium is murdered, the District Attorney's Special Investigator, "Bonnie" Dundee must go undercover to find the killer. Were any of the inmates of the asylum insane enough to have committed the crime? Or, was it one of the staff, motivated by jealousy? And what was is the secret in the murdered man's past. Find the answer in . . . **One Drop of Blood**

AVAILABLE FROM RESURRECTED PRESS!

GEMS OF MYSTERY
LOST JEWELS FROM A MORE ELEGANT AGE

Three wonderful tales of mystery from some of the best known writers of the period before the First World War -

A foggy London night, a Russian princess who steals jewels, a corpse; a mysterious murder, an opera singer, and stolen pearls; two young people who crash a masked ball only to find themselves caught up in a daring theft of jewels; these are the subjects of this collection of entertaining tales of love, jewels, and mystery. This collection includes:

- **In the Fog - by Richard Harding Davis's**

- **The Affair at the Hotel Semiramis - by A.E.W. Mason**

- **Hearts and Masks - Harold MacGrath**

AVAILABLE FROM RESURRECTED PRESS!

THE EDWARDIAN DETECTIVES
LITERARY SLEUTHS OF THE EDWARDIAN ERA

The exploits of the great Victorian Detectives, Poe's C. Auguste Dupin, Gaboriau's Lecoq, and most famously, Arthur Conan Doyle's Sherlock Holmes, are well known. But what of those fictional detectives that came after, those of the Edwardian Age? The period between the death of Queen Victoria and the First World War had been called the Golden Age of the detective short story, but how familiar is the modern reader with the sleuths of this era? And such an extraordinary group they were, including in their numbers an unassuming English priest, a blind man, a master of disguises, a lecturer in medical jurisprudence, a noble woman working for Scotland Yard, and a savant so brilliant he was known as "The Thinking Machine."

To introduce readers to these detectives, Resurrected Press has assembled a collection of stories featuring these and other remarkable sleuths in The Edwardian Detectives.

- The Case of Laker, Absconded by Arthur Morrison
- The Fenchurch Street Mystery by Baroness Orczy
- The Crime of the French Café by Nick Carter
- The Man with Nailed Shoes by R Austin Freeman
- The Blue Cross by G. K. Chesterton
- The Case of the Pocket Diary Found in the Snow by Augusta Groner
- The Ninescore Mystery by Baroness Orczy
- The Riddle of the Ninth Finger by Thomas W. Hanshew
- The Knight's Cross Signal Problem by Ernest Bramah

- The Problem of Cell 13 by Jacques Futrelle
- The Conundrum of the Golf Links by Percy James Brebner
- The Silkworms of Florence by Clifford Ashdown
- The Gateway of the Monster by William Hope Hodgson
- The Affair at the Semiramis Hotel by A. E. W. Mason
- The Affair of the Avalanche Bicycle & Tyre Co., LTD by Arthur Morrison

RESURRECTED PRESS CLASSIC MYSTERY CATALOGUE

Journeys into Mystery
Travel and Mystery in a More Elegant Time

The Edwardian Detectives
Literary Sleuths of the Edwardian Era

Gems of Mystery
Lost Jewels from a More Elegant Age

E. C. Bentley
Trent's Last Case: The Woman in Black

Ernest Bramah
Max Carrados Resurrected:
The Detective Stories of Max Carrados

Agatha Christie
The Secret Adversary
The Mysterious Affair at Styles

Octavus Roy Cohen
Midnight

Freeman Wills Croft
The Ponson Case
The Pit Prop Syndicate

J. S. Fletcher
The Herapath Property
The Rayner-Slade Amalgamation
The Chestermarke Instinct
The Paradise Mystery
Dead Men's Money

The Middle of Things
Ravensdene Court
Scarhaven Keep
The Orange-Yellow Diamond
The Middle Temple Murder
The Tallyrand Maxim
The Borough Treasurer
In the Mayor's Parlour
The Saftey Pin

R. Austin Freeman
*The Mystery of 31 New Inn from the Dr. Thorndyke
Series*
*John Thorndyke's Cases from the Dr. Thorndyke
Series*
The Red Thumb Mark from The Dr. Thorndyke Series
The Eye of Osiris from The Dr. Thorndyke Series
A Silent Witness from the Dr. John Thorndyke Series
The Cat's Eye from the Dr. John Thorndyke Series
*Helen Vardon's Confession: A Dr. John Thorndyke
Story*
As a Thief in the Night: A Dr. John Thorndyke Story
*Mr. Pottermack's Oversight: A Dr. John Thorndyke
Story*
*Dr. Thorndyke Intervenes: A Dr. John Thorndyke
Story*
The Singing Bone: The Adventures of Dr. Thorndyke
The Stoneware Monkey: A Dr. John Thorndyke Story
*The Great Portrait Mystery, and Other Stories: A
Collection of Dr. John Thorndyke and Other Stories*
The Penrose Mystery: A Dr. John Thorndyke Story
The Uttermost Farthing: A Savant's Vendetta

Arthur Griffiths
The Passenger From Calais
The Rome Express

Fergus Hume
The Mystery of a Hansom Cab
The Green Mummy
The Silent House
The Secret Passage

Edgar Jepson
The Loudwater Mystery

A. E. W. Mason
At the Villa Rose

A. A. Milne
The Red House Mystery
Baroness Emma Orczy
The Old Man in the Corner

Edgar Allan Poe
The Detective Stories of Edgar Allan Poe

Arthur J. Rees
The Hampstead Mystery
The Shrieking Pit
The Hand In The Dark
The Moon Rock
The Mystery of the Downs

Mary Roberts Rinehart
Sight Unseen and The Confession

Dorothy L. Sayers
Whose Body?

Sir William Magnay
The Hunt Ball Mystery

Mabel and Paul Thorne
The Sheridan Road Mystery

Louis Tracy
The Strange Case of Mortimer Fenley
The Albert Gate Mystery
The Bartlett Mystery
The Postmaster's Daughter
The House of Peril
The Sandling Case: What Would You Have Done?
Charles Edmonds Walk
The Paternoster Ruby

John R. Watson
The Mystery of the Downs
The Hampstead Mystery

Edgar Wallace
The Daffodil Mystery
The Crimson Circle

Carolyn Wells
Vicky Van
The Man Who Fell Through the Earth
In the Onyx Lobby
Raspberry Jam
The Clue
The Room with the Tassels
The Vanishing of Betty Varian
The Mystery Girl
The White Alley
The Curved Blades
Anybody but Anne
The Bride of a Moment
Faulkner's Folly
The Diamond Pin
The Gold Bag
The Mystery of the Sycamore
The Come Back

Raoul Whitfield
Death in a Bowl

And much more!
Visit ResurrectedPress.com
for our complete catalogue

About Resurrected Press

A division of Intrepid Ink, LLC, Resurrected Press is dedicated to bringing high quality, vintage books back into publication. See our entire catalogue and find out more at www.ResurrectedPress.com.

About Intrepid Ink, LLC

Intrepid Ink, LLC provides full publishing services to authors of fiction and non-fiction books, eBooks and websites. From editing to formatting, from publishing to marketing, Intrepid Ink gets your creative works into the hands of the people who want to read them. Find out more at www.IntrepidInk.com.

www.ingramcontent.com/pod-product-compliance
Lightning Source LLC
Chambersburg PA
CBHW071329250626
47159CB00004B/1530